After the Embers

A Clean, Slow-Burn Romance About Broken Promises, New Beginnings, and the Power of Forgiveness

By

Seraphine Moonwater

Get bonus scenes, sneak peeks, deleted scenes and early access to the next book.

☞ ☞ Tap here: https://wrongblacklove.com/join-the-journey/

Or scan the QR code below:

TABLE OF CONTENTS

CHAPTER 1: FELL SWOOP

The grocery bags rustled as I spread them across the counter, flipping open my notepad for what had to be the twentieth time. It was another day of shopping for ingredients I would probably never use again.

I had everything accounted for: flour, maple syrup, apples, and some questionable-looking herbs that the farmer had assured me were "essential" for an authentic Vermont stew. I wouldn't have known; I had barely cooked back home.

Still, I spent two days off from the hospital preparing for that night—this absurdly ambitious Vermont dinner party meant to prove that I, Imara Hastings, could survive in that town and thrive in it.

Outside, the wind howled, rattling against the windows like it had a personal vendetta. Vermont had gotten colder, biting through my coat every time I stepped outside. My boots were lined up neatly by the door, still covered in a fine dusting of slush.

I tightened my grip on the pen, scanning my list again. Pot roast? Check. Mashed potatoes? Check. Confidence? Absolutely not.

My phone dinged from the counter. Then again. Then, a third time, each chime was more insistent than the last. I swiped it open, narrowing my eyes at the group chat that Charlotte had made for all of us—fittingly titled "The Inner Circle."

Linda said, "Hey, so slight problem... don't panic... but I think I have come down with something."

Caroline replied, "Wait... I feel awful, too. Like, really awful."

Charlotte exclaimed, "WHAT THE HECK. I am in bed trying not to drench the sheets in mucus."

I stared at the screen, rereading the messages as dread pooled in my stomach. No. No, no, no. I said, "You're joking. Are you guys playing a prank on me because it's NOT FUNNY?"

Linda said, "I wish I was. I have a fever, chills, the works."

Caroline replied, "I thought I was just tired, but no. Vermont flu has gotten me."

Charlotte exclaimed, "This was a betrayal. I was single-handedly ready to save your dinner party from disaster."

I pinched the bridge of my nose, inhaling sharply. "So you're all telling me that the Vermont flue has wiped out my entire cooking support system in one fell swoop?"

Caroline replied, "That's a dramatic way to put it, but... yeah."

Linda asked, "Soooo... what is the backup plan?"

Backup plan. Right. I let my gaze drift over the kitchen, imagining the chaos that would ensue if I attempted this solo: pots overflowing, smoke alarms blaring, and someone calling the fire department before I got the potatoes on the stove. There was no backup plan, meaning I had to call the whole thing off or find more help.

I sighed and momentarily pressed my forehead against the cool countertop before straightening up. The smart thing to do would have been to postpone. Canceling made me feel like a failure, and I refused to let some flu-stricken friends and my culinary incompetence take me down that easily. Postponing felt dangerously close to giving up. And I hated the idea of that.

I trudged toward my bedroom, peeling off my sweater and tossing it onto the chair in the corner. The wind outside relentlessly rattled against the windowpane, but it had nothing on the thoughts circling in my head.

While I prided myself on many things, culinary excellence was not one of them. The thought of my guests politely choking down whatever disaster I plated up sent a fresh wave of anxiety rolling through me.

YouTube tutorials weren't cutting it. Recipe blogs? Who even trusted those? They always said, "Just follow the steps," but somehow, mine never turned out like the pictures.

I turned onto my side, staring at the soft glow of my alarm clock. The red numbers blurred slightly, my body finally giving in to exhaustion, but the last thing on my mind before sleep pulled me under was the dinner party—and the real possibility of disaster.

That morning, Mrs. Carter was in fine form: she was super grumpy, demanding, and extra unimpressed with the hospital's so-called hospitality.

"I don't know why you people insist on serving that godawful excuse of oatmeal," she huffed, arms crossed over her chest as I checked her blood pressure. "It tasted like damp cardboard. Where was my tea?"

I bit back a smile. "You know, I could sneak in some sugar packets if that is what it takes to get you off my case. You can't have watery tea every morning, Mrs. Carter."

She narrowed her eyes at me, unimpressed. "I don't need sugar. I need edible food."

I chuckled under my breath, scribbling her vitals into the chart. "Fair enough."

She watched me for a beat, then tilted her head. "So. How is that little dinner party of yours coming along?"

I sighed, glancing up. "It was coming along fine... until my entire guest list dropped like flies. Apparently, the flu is making its way through The Inner Circle."

"Ooo, I heard it's a bad one."

I nodded.

"All sniffling, sneezing, and quarantining. And now I am stuck doing this alone, with cooking skills that anyone would generously describe as tragic."

Mrs. Carter hummed, leaning back against her pillows like she was settling into a plan. "So, no backup. No friends to bail you out."

"None," I muttered, flipping her chart closed. "I should probably just cancel."

"Oh, don't be ridiculous."

Her tone sharpened with purpose. "You have options."

I raised a brow. "Unless Vermont has a rent-a-chef hotline you haven't told me about, I truly don't have that many options."

A slow smile—the kind of smile that made my stomach clench with foreboding— curled across her face.

"What you need," she said sweetly, "is Noah."

I blinked. "Excuse me?"

"My grandson," she said, as if I didn't already know that. "You know, he owns his own café, knows his way around a kitchen, and wouldn't let you destroy a perfectly good meal."

I stared at her, waiting for the punchline. It didn't come.

"Mrs. Carter," I said carefully, "with all due respect, your grandson and I didn't exactly... get along."

She waved a hand, unimpressed. "You argued over cinnamon. Big deal."

I exhaled through my nose. "It was a big deal. He snatched the last one right out from under me!"

"And then he gave it to you," she said pointedly. "Grumbling the whole time, but still."

"He gave it to me like he was surrendering a kidney. It was dramatic."

"So were you," she fired back. "The point was that Noah didn't have to give it to you. But he did."

"Mrs. Carter," I said slowly, "even if I was desperate enough to ask—which I wasn't—he is probably too busy to help with a... minuscule house dinner."

"He isn't too busy," she said with absolute certainty. "Especially not for me. And he likes a challenge."

"This isn't a challenge. It is a suicide mission."

Her eyes glinted. "Then it is perfect for him."

I groaned, rubbing my forehead. "This is a terrible idea."

"What is terrible," she said with that steel-soft tone, "is giving up on something you care about just because asking for help makes your pride twitch."

I glanced down at her chart, pretending to double-check something on it, all so I could avoid looking her in the eye. I hated how right she was. Again.

I should have said no. I should have told her there was absolutely no way I would willingly interact with Noah Carter again, especially not in a setting where he got to judge my cooking and probably my entire existence.

But Mrs. Carter had the kind of authority that demanded obedience, and somehow, by the time I finished my rounds, I found myself walking out of her room having—against all reason—agreed to ask him for help.

Under duress. Obviously.

CHAPTER 2: EDIBLE

The bells above the door chimed as I stepped inside, and the warm scent of freshly baked bread and cinnamon wrapped around me like a cozy ambush.

It was after work. I was exhausted, still in my scrubs, and the thought of asking Noah Carter for help clashed violently with every bone in my stubborn, pride-ridden body. I shouldn't have been here. I didn't want to be here. Every instinct within me screamed to turn around and pretend I had gotten the wrong address.

Noah's café was infuriatingly nice. Its mix of rustic wooden tables, soft lighting, and the faint hum of jazz playing in the background gave it that effortless charm that made you want to settle in for hours. It was like a Vermont postcard brought to life.

I had been to the café once or twice with Charlotte, but that time felt different because I hadn't realized it was his. Then I realized it was his, and suddenly, I noticed everything: the cookbooks by Black chefs lining the shelf above the espresso machine, the framed photo of an old soul food joint tucked in the corner, the subtle nods to his heritage layered into every detail. The warm spices. The music. The art.

It was cool, really cool. It was the kind of place that didn't just serve food but told a story: Noah's story. Not that I was there to admire it.

I marched toward the counter, determined and focused on a mission. I would ask Noah for help, and he would say yes (because Mrs. Carter was terrifying, and he wouldn't dare disobey her). I would be out of there in five minutes.

A girl with a perky ponytail and a bright, way too chipper smile greeted me. "Good morning! What can I get started for you?"

I hesitated. "Uh... is Noah here?"

Her brows lifted slightly, and I saw a little flicker of interest in her eyes.

"Yeah," she said, recovering with a quick smile. "He's in the back. Want me to grab him?"

I nodded, resisting the urge to sink into the floor from sheer secondhand awkwardness. There was nothing casual about this. I felt like I had just walked into someone's inner sanctum and asked for the dragon by name.

She disappeared through the swinging door, and I braced myself.

A few moments later, the door swung open again, and there he was: Noah Carter, in all his smug, infuriatingly attractive glory, flour dusted on his sleeves, sleeves pushed up to his elbows, a towel slung over his shoulder like he was starring in some Vermont bachelor ad.

He leaned against the counter when he saw me, a flicker of surprise crossing his face before his smile settled into a slow smirk as he crossed his arms over his chest.

"Well, well. Look who finally decided to stop by," Noah said, tilting his head slightly. "Didn't expect to see you here. Shouldn't you be preparing for your dinner?"

I arched a brow, stepping closer to the counter, the scent of roasted coffee and fresh herbs wrapped around me. "Hard to prepare for a dinner when your entire guest list is down with the plague and your only backup plan involves setting something on fire."

He pretended to consider that, propping one elbow casually on the counter. "Sounds like a bold menu."

I crossed my arms, letting my eyes wander briefly over the warm glow of the pendant lights above us and the quiet clink of dishes from somewhere in the back. "Mrs. Carter said you could help."

That earned me an actual pause. Noah's brow lifted ever so slightly, just enough to say I had his attention.

"She did, did she? Well, I already gave the best advice: maple syrup."

I blinked at him, deadpan. "Right. Because drenching everything in maple is the clear solution to all my problems, right? Noah, she thinks you're my best shot at not poisoning anyone, but hey, maybe I'll just glaze the chicken in syrup and call it a day."

He muttered something under his breath—probably about his grandmother—and rubbed the back of his neck. I caught the momentary hesitation in his posture; it looked like he was genuinely debating it. But then—

"Look," he said, straightening, "I'd love to help your little situation, but I've got a lot on my plate right now, pun not intended." His mouth twitched like he was half-proud of the joke. "I'm already stretched thin, and teaching you how not to burn down your kitchen isn't exactly in the schedule."

Ouch.

I sucked in a breath, leveling him with a look. "What if I paid you?"

He leaned back against the counter again and folded his arms across his chest like he was bracing himself. Behind him, a slow jazz track hummed through the café, warm and lazy, completely at odds with the tension gathering between us.

"Still sounds like a time commitment," he said.

"You sound like someone doing his best and trying as hard as possible not to get involved."

His eyes flickered to mine. "Maybe I am."

There was a beat of taut and charged silence before I shrugged.

"Fine," I said, with a shrug that masked more nerves than I'd like to admit. "I'll figure it out. Burnt stew, half-cooked chicken, complete humiliation; it's all part of the charm, right?"

As I turned toward the door, the soft creak of the wooden floor under my boots was the only sound between us.

"You can explain to Mrs. Carter why I crashed and burned," I tossed over my shoulder. "I am sure she'll be very understanding."

His dramatic and exasperated sigh was loud enough to stop me mid-step.

"Fine! If you have to, come back after closing," he said.

I glanced back just in time to catch the look on his face: a perfect storm of resignation and reluctant amusement. His tone made it sound like I had personally ruined his entire week.

I smiled. Bright. Unbothered. Maybe even a little smug. "Great. Looking forward to it."

I tugged my coat tighter around me, trying not to shiver as I waited outside. My breath fogged up the glass, and for a second, I considered turning around. I could have just gone home, ordered takeout, or even faked a power outage.

But then the lock clicked, and the door swung open.

Noah stood in the doorway, still in that damn apron, arms crossed, his expression somewhere between amused and unreadable.

"Well, well," he drawled. "You actually showed."

I stepped inside, trying not to notice how nice the place looked in the low light—or how nice he looked in it.

"I said I would. Didn't I?" I said.

He lifted a brow.

"I figured you'd back out once you realized I wouldn't do all the work for you."

I dropped my bag onto a nearby stool and narrowed my eyes.

"You seem to have a lot of assumptions about me."

"And so far, I've been right." He pushed off the counter, grabbed another apron from the hook, and tossed it in my direction.

"Let's get this over with."

Charming.

It started fine—on paper, anyway. He ran through the basics like he was giving a cooking class on a mildly budgeted YouTube channel. He explained how to properly dice an onion (which apparently didn't mean crying your way through it), the difference between a simmer and a boil (yes, there was a difference), and why eyeballing seasoning "like some reckless amateur" was practically a sin in his kitchen.

He said "reckless amateur" while looking directly at me, and I tried not to stab him with the paring knife.

Then came the flour. I was scooping it into a bowl, trying my best to look competent, but my hand jerked just slightly. It was not my fault; the bag was awkward, or perhaps gravity had shifted. What mattered was the result: a small cloud of white dust exploded across the counter and landed all over Noah's sleeve.

We both froze.

I clasped a hand over my mouth, not because I was trying to be polite, but because I was two seconds from laughing. Noah exhaled slowly, brushing flour off his arm.

"You know, most people wait at least twenty minutes before initiating kitchen warfare," he remarked.

I snorted.

"It wasn't on purpose."

"Mm-hmm," he muttered, looking entirely unconvinced. I glanced at the counter—covered in flour, onions, half-diced herbs, and now a truly unfortunate streak of butter across my apron—and exhaled.

"I was going to wear a ratty t-shirt for this," I mumbled, half to myself.

"What stopped you?" he asked without looking up.

I hesitated. "You." I thought to myself.

I trimmed my hair twice, and now I was standing in his café trying not to look like I actually cared.

"Laundry," I lied.

He glanced up, and there was something in his eyes—something quieter than his usual smirk—but it disappeared as quickly as it had come.

"I like cinnamon," I argued, tossing a little extra into the dough mixture just to be petty.

Noah made a noise as if I had personally insulted his entire profession.

"That wasn't liking cinnamon; that was ruining the recipe's balance."

I rolled my eyes.

"Balance. Right."

He glared; I smirked. And somehow, between all the bickering, the mess, the complete and utter failure that was my first lesson, I couldn't help but watch how way he moved, completely at ease in the kitchen, the way he talked about flavors like they were second nature, his hands working with practiced precision—it was frustrating. And annoyingly attractive.

I shoved that thought aside immediately and instead crossed my arms as I watched him fix my ruined dough with an annoyingly smug ease.

"So, what was the next lesson, Sensei?" I asked.

He didn't even look up.

"Next lesson? You haven't even passed this one," he replied.

I scowled, and he smirked. By some miracle—and with a suspicious amount of hovering on his part—I managed to pull together something that resembled food. Not a dessert this time, but an actual dish: Vermont cheddar and herb biscuits.

Okay, so he had given me precise, hand-holding-level instructions, and yes, he ended up re-measuring my ingredients behind my back. Still, the biscuits came out golden and fluffy and didn't taste like total disappointment.

I beamed as I pulled them from the oven, carefully transferring them to a cooling rack while Noah leaned on the counter, arms folded like a judge on some overly dramatic cooking show.

"Not bad," he admitted after taking a bite and chewing with the seriousness of a man deciding my fate. "Surprisingly... edible."

"Wow," I deadpanned. "High praise from the king of smug."

He chuckled, but his chuckle was faint and distracted. I caught him glancing at the wall clock, and just like that, the small sense of pride I was beginning to feel took a nosedive.

"I'll send you the rest of my recipes," he said, pushing off the counter. "Dinner's in what? Four days? I don't have time to do this again before then."

Even though I had seen it coming, something in me deflated.

"Right. Of course," I said quickly, busying myself with wiping flour off the already clean counter. "I know you are busy. You have a whole café to run and a reputation to maintain."

He grabbed a dish towel, ran it through his hands, and avoided my eyes.

"It isn't that I don't want to help. I just... can't promise more time right now," he explained.

"It is fine," I replied, way too fast. "Really. The recipes are more than enough. I'll figure it out."

He nodded and headed toward the door, flicking the lights off in the back.

"You will do fine," he assured me.

I stood in the middle of the kitchen, surrounded by the lingering scent of cheddar and thyme, wondering why his words sounded more like a dismissal than encouragement.

It was fine. I didn't need his help anyway. Right?

CHAPTER 3: MATCHMAKER

Two days before the dinner party, I had officially hit the point where even boiling water felt like a gamble.

The notes Noah had sent me might as well have been in Latin because whenever I attempted something from his overly confident recipe list, it ended in either smoke, sadness, or a culinary identity crisis.

Still, I told myself I was fine—that I didn't need him, that this whole dinner was my idea, and that I'd figure it out myself. Thank you very much.

That illusion lasted precisely until I got a text from the hospital front desk: "Mrs. Carter isn't feeling well. She's asking for you specifically."

That triggered my panic.

By the time I got there—with my coat barely buttoned and my stethoscope in hand—I was running on instinct and half a granola bar. But the moment I stepped into her room, I stopped short because I found Noah by her side, hands on his hip, staring down at his grandmother.

"Mrs. Carter?" I called, a little oblivious, still in nurse mode. "What's wrong? How are you feeling?"

Mrs. Carter, traitorous and not even bothering to look apologetic, perked up in bed as though she had just returned from the brink. "Well, look at that. My two favorite people together. Isn't this convenient?"

I narrowed my eyes. "You're fine."

"I'm eighty-two and surrounded by amateurs," she sniffed. "Fine is relative."

Noah muttered something under his breath that sounded suspiciously dramatic, and I swear she heard it but chose to focus on her grand performance instead.

"Since you're both here," she said primly while folding her hands, "I was hoping you could run a few errands for me. Nothing too difficult; just a couple of things from town. And I need that farmer's market tea that doesn't taste like the hospital floor."

"You want both of us to go?"

Noah pushed off the wall, clearly not thrilled. "Pretty sure one of us could handle it just fine."

"I'm sure one of you could," she replied, arching a brow in that "watch your tone, young man" way she had perfected over the last eighty-something years. "But you," she said as she pointed at Noah, "aren't a woman. You don't understand the art of shopping. You rush. You miss things, return with the wrong tea, and act like I'm the problem."

He opened his mouth, then closed it again.

"I can't just... leave, Mrs. Carter. I'm at work, clocked in—"

"I've already had your schedule cleared. I spoke to that nice doctor you work with. What's his name? The one with the good teeth."

"Dr. Whitaker," I muttered, already regretting the entire interaction.

"Wait! You talked to him?"

Mrs. Carter waved a hand as if it were no big deal. "He stopped by earlier to check on me. I may have mentioned that you looked like you could use a little fresh air, but I said something about how a bit of time out of the hospital would do you good."

"You framed it like a mental health concern, didn't you?" I asked flatly.

"I framed it like self-care," she replied primly. "And the good doctor agreed. He said he didn't see the harm if you completed your rounds."

"I—Mrs. Carter, that isn't how things work here. I can't just—"

But she waved a hand as though she were bored. "You're here, you're healthy, you've got legs. I need my errands done. It's cold, I'm old, and the hospital tea tastes like regret."

Before either of us could get another word in, she shoved a folded piece of paper into my hand: it was a handwritten list, front and back—of course.

"You wouldn't make an old woman do this herself, would you?" She sighed dramatically, sinking further into her pillows as if the mere mention of effort had drained the little strength she had left.

I clenched my jaw, my eyes darting to the list. Noah snorted under his breath, clearly amused, and then—exuding all the smugness of someone who knew he wasn't the one holding the paper—offered a theatrical little bow and motioned toward the door.

We silently made it to the truck, the doors slamming shut like punctuation marks as we got it.

"I was supposed to meet a supplier at ten. I have three orders due this afternoon. I have bread proofing, and if Marcus touches the croissants again, I swear—" He cut off, already dialing his phone. "I'll be five minutes late. Or twenty. Depends on how long shopping for scents takes."

I stared out the window, clutching the list in my lap, and sighed in anticipation for what promised to be a long errand.

The farmers' market was quiet that day; the patrons were mostly locals wearing thick coats and weatherproof boots, moving briskly between booths like they'd done it a hundred times (probably because they had).

Noah walked a step ahead of me, glancing at the stalls with mild disinterest as if he'd memorized the entire layout. He had already called the bakery twice, and it had only been fifteen minutes.

We stopped at a small wooden stall with a handwritten sign that simply said "Peanut" in blocky, fading letters. A wiry man with laugh lines and a stained flannel shirt grinned when he spotted us.

"Well, well," he said, squinting at Noah. "Let me guess—Mrs. Carter finally ran you outta the bakery to fetch her miracle tea?"

Noah blinked. "Miracle tea?"

Peanut chuckled and turned to me. "You're her nurse friend? She told me someone might come by for the moringa blend. Said to make sure it was the one in the brown paper bag—not the plastic pouch, 'cause the plastic made it taste like dust. Her words, not mine."

I nodded slowly, glancing at Noah. "She never sent you here before?"

"Nope." He sounded mildly offended. "She's complained about my chamomile but has never said anything about a miracle tea."

Peanut shrugged and handed me the bag. "Well, she's getting picky with age. Bless her."

I tucked it carefully into the tote bag and thanked him, already wondering what else she was secretly sourcing from vendors—as though she were running a black market side hustle.

There was a bit of traffic as we headed to the next stop on Mrs. Carter's Great Vermont Scavenger Hunt. Noah drummed his fingers against the steering wheel, glancing sideways at me between red lights as if he was busy trying to figure something out.

Eventually, he said, "Why did she like you so much?"

"What?" I asked.

"I mean," he shrugged—still not looking at me—"she barely tolerated most people. But she wouldn't shut up about you. You brought her tea and checked on her more than her nurses did, and now she has us running errands together."

"I don't know why Mrs. Carter likes me. I thought it was just because I let her have her jabs—and sometimes even threw one at her. She is a sweet lady, as sweet as unsweetened grapefruit juice."

He snorted and moved on to our next stop, the bakery.

"Sorry," the woman behind the counter said, smiling sympathetically. "If it was the rye twist you were after, we sold out hours ago. Mrs. Carter said her nurse lady friend would come in for it, but you were a tad bit late."

Noah groaned. "You've got to be kidding me."

"Well," I said, glancing over at him, "weren't you supposed to be the guy who baked everything from scratch with magic hands and a smug attitude? Couldn't you just whip up a rye twist?"

He snorted. "It isn't a spell, Imara. It takes time. And ingredients. And—"

"Effort?" I cut in sweetly.

He shot me a look. "No. Respect."

I grinned, enjoying it far too much. "So you're telling me you've got all this culinary talent, but you're going to let an eighty-something-year-old woman down because you're too proud to make her favorite bread?"

He glared ahead, his jaw ticking. "You're manipulative. Rye twist takes time—which I no longer have because I spent it all shopping with you."

He exhaled sharply, muttering something that sounded like "unbelievable," but I caught the corner of his mouth twitching as if he were trying not to smile.

We walked in a comfortable silence for a moment, our boots crunching on thin patches of ice on the sidewalk. It wasn't an awkward silence—it was easy and comfortable, if I was honest (which I wasn't, not with myself, not at that moment).

Our last stop was a general store that looked un-updated since the 1950s. It was charming if you were into that sort of thing, but it was less appealing when you were trying to decipher a grocery list written in what I could only describe as Victorian-era calligraphy.

I held up the crumpled note, squinting. "Was this... turmeric? Or tamarind?"

Noah leaned over my shoulder, equally confused. We spent ten full minutes arguing about whether the third word was "bay leaves" or "beef liver," crouching in the spice aisle as though it were a puzzle only the worthy could solve.

At one point, he simply handed the note to the cashier and asked, "Do you speak retired nurse with a superiority complex?"

Miraculously, we managed to cobble together everything on the list—more or less—and headed outside with our bags.

That's when we spotted an elderly man, hunched and clearly struggling to lift his grocery bags into the trunk of his car. He dropped a can, cursed softly, and tried to bend over for it.

I didn't even think—I just moved, reaching for the can and steadying the wobbling bag on his arm.

Noah was beside me seconds later, quietly lifting the heavier bags and nudging the trunk open with one elbow as if it were pure muscle memory.

Thanks to teamwork, we had the car packed in no time. The man beamed, reaching out to shake both of our hands with a warm "Thank you, kids" before driving off with a shaky little wave.

I glanced at Noah, whose expression was unreadable as he watched the taillights disappear.

"Let's get out of here. This scavenger hunt is over, and I need to get back to my café," he said.

CHAPTER 4: QUALITY CONTROL

My fridge was full of ingredients I had only recently learned how to pronounce, and my counters still looked like a cooking show audition that hadn't made the final cut—but the dough was rising properly that time, and I hadn't set off the smoke alarm.

Progress.

My phone buzzed while I was mentally organizing my game plan— half out loud, half in my head. It was Mom and Dad.

I hovered for a second, thumb in the air. I could have let it ring out and claimed I was elbow-deep in poultry prep, but guilt won (as usual), and I swiped to answer.

"Imara, tell your father Pilates is for everyone."

"Uh, hi to you, too, Mom?"

In the background, I heard Dad's voice.

"Your mother is already beautiful. She doesn't need those classes."

"Dad, I'm sure she wants to go for mobility and core strength, not for your approval," I replied, already sliding into referee mode.

"She also wants to wear those tights to class," he added dryly. "Those are only for me."

"Okay, ew." I scrubbed a hand down my face. "Mom. Dad. Please. Can we talk about literally anything else?"

Mom laughed.

"Your father's just mad I still look better in leggings than he does."

I paused mid-cringe.

"Wait—since when do you wear leggings?"

"I never said that," Dad said, ignoring my question. "I said you're distracting. As someone has pointed out, distractions aren't helpful in group settings."

I groaned.

"Is this what parenthood does to people?"

Mom sighed, but there was warmth in it.

"Only if you're lucky enough to fall in love with your best friend."

Okay. Cute. Still gross.

"Anyway," she said, switching gears, "How's the dinner planning going? Are you surviving, or should I ship you backup rolls and moral support?"

I glanced around my kitchen, which looked like a Food Network challenge set halfway through the round: there were bowls everywhere, dough proving, and a roast marinating in a Ziploc bag that kept threatening to leak. And yet... it wasn't a disaster. I smiled, tucking the phone between my shoulder and ear to free up my hands so I could start mincing some garlic.

"Actually... not terrible. I'm managing. Slowly. Messily. But managing."

Dad chimed in again.

"That's our girl."

I dropped the garlic into a pan already sizzling with butter and reached for the thyme.

"The biscuits are ready, the glaze is cooling, and I'm only bleeding a tiny bit from that earlier potato peeler incident."

Mom gasped.

"Imara—"

"Kidding. Mostly."

I turned my attention to trimming green beans for blanching, making a mental note to chill the wine in the next half hour. I had a spreadsheet, a printed-out schedule, and a color-coded post-it note system that even Charlotte would have approved of. And that was a good thing, too, because my intimate dinner party had somehow turned into friends plus friends plus random extras from town who had heard about the biscuits.

"Your dad and I were just talking about how much fun you seemed to be having," she said, casual but definitely fishing. "We were joking that you might not come back at all."

I glanced up, already suspicious.

"So..." she drew the word out, sing-song sweet, "when are you coming back?"

I paused for a second.

"I mean," she added, still in that light, too-cheerful tone, "this is starting to sound a little... permanent."

"You know I'm supposed to be here for at least six months," I added after a beat. "It's only been three. I still have some time to go, and then I can decide if I'm—"

"It's Vermont," Dad cut in. "It's not home."

Mom's voice returned, softer this time.

"You know we're proud of you, right? We just... we didn't think you'd stay so long."

I bit my lip, rolling out dough with a bit more force than necessary.

"I know." And I did.

I glanced around the kitchen—my kitchen, even if it was mine just for now—with its cluttered counters, half-finished prep, and the faint scent of maple and thyme drifting through the air... and part of me wondered if that was still true.

Maybe it was because I had put in the effort there. Because I wanted it to work. Because for the first time, I felt like I was part of something and like I belonged. And maybe that was my fault. Maybe it was selfish. I felt guilty even thinking about it.

"I'm coming back," I said quickly, forcing the words out before I could second-guess them. "I promise."

They sounded a little more relaxed after that, but I could still hear the worry tucked behind my mom's layered advice and the unspoken ache in my dad's awkward silence before we hung up. I placed the phone gently on the counter, dusted my hands with flour, and kept moving.

While running on too little sleep and way too much caffeine, I rounded the corner to Mrs. Carter's room, her chart in one hand and my sanity barely clinging on in the other. I paused just outside the doorway when I heard voices drifting out.

"She's finally stopped bringing me that dishwater tea," Mrs. Carter announced as smugly as ever. "I mean, the poor girl didn't know— bless her heart—and it wasn't her fault these dimwits didn't know how to boil water."

"This new blend?" she continued as if she were on a Food Network review show. "It's got actual flavor. Imagine that."

"I'll be sure to pass that glowing review along," Noah replied dryly.

Noah. My stomach did that flip it usually did at the thought of him; it really needed to stop doing so.

"Ma—hold on, do they even know you are drinking this?"

"Boy, hush, moringa is good for everything. Are you going to snitch on me now?"

"I would if you I didn't have actual things to do, like run a café."

"It's Vermont, not New York," she snorted. "Today was as busy as my schedule."

There was a beat, and then Mrs. Carter lowered her voice to what she thought was a whisper.

"By the way, has our little cooking crisis improved?"

"I could only help her out once, Ma. She did... well enough the first time. I was sure she'd catch up on her own."

"One time?" She slapped him so hard that I nearly jumped out of the corner.

Noah flinched and cradled his arm, eyes wide.

"Ma! Are you serious right now?"

"Is that how I raised you? Oh my goodness, Noah, were you trying to embarrass me in front of the poor sweet girl?"

"I was helpful," he muttered. "But the café wouldn't run itself. I had actual things to do."

Mrs. Carter waved him off with all the grace of a royal decree.

"Please. I raised you with two hands and no sleep. You can handle a little multitasking."

I leaned against the doorframe, biting back a smile.

"Sounds like you'd been very well-trained, Noah. Did you just choose your own way?"

Noah nearly jumped when I spoke, his head snapping toward the door as if someone had caught him stealing government secrets instead of being emotionally terrorized by a ninety-year-old with a tea obsession. Mrs. Carter beamed as if I'd just handed her a gold medal.

"See? She got it."

I strode the rest of the way into the room with zero remorse. Noah chuckled from the chair near her bedside, and although I did not look directly at him, I could feel him there, relaxed, legs stretched out. Noah sighed as if he had aged twenty years in the last five minutes.

"I'm leaving before she ropes me into alphabetizing her tea."

"You can't leave," Mrs. Carter said, lifting her chin like royalty. "I need that cinnamon chai from the café—the one you only make on Thursdays. And while you are at it, pick up those meat pies from that bakery Imara likes."

I blinked.

"Wait, how did you know—"

Mrs. Carter grinned.

"My grandson here—"

"Okay!" Noah cut in louder than necessary. "That is enough commentary for today, Ma."

"I also thought maybe the two of you could revisit that sad little menu of yours while you were here. It needs fixing."

"Mrs. Carter, you are always busy meddling. I was working, and my menu is coming out perfect, actually," I said, gesturing to my ID badge as though it meant something in that room.

"Perfect, huh? That's a bold claim. What have you done so far besides not setting your oven on fire?"

I tossed him a smug smile.

"Wouldn't you like to know?"

"I would, actually," he said, crossing his arms and leaning a little too comfortably against the doorframe. "I was picturing probably way too much thyme. Maybe a charred pan or two."

I rolled my eyes.

"Well, I guess you'd just have to come to the dinner party and find out."

The words were out before I could stop them. Oh no. Noah's brows lifted. His eyes widened slightly in surprise, not the 'how dare you' kind, but more of a 'wait, are you serious?' kind. Before I could backpedal, Mrs. Carter lit up like she'd been waiting for that precise moment.

"Perfect. Noah will be there."

I whipped around.

"That was not an invitation."

"It was," she said smugly. "And I accepted on his behalf."

I turned to Noah, hoping he would correct her by rolling his eyes and saying something snarky like, 'Absolutely not attending your dinner party.' Instead, he just shrugged. He shrugged. My eyes narrowed.

"Seriously?"

He glanced up, nonchalant.

"Purely for quality control."

Mrs. Carter beamed, victorious. I swear I heard distant thunder, or maybe that was just the sound of me spiraling.

CHAPTER 5: BOLDER AND DARKER

Against all odds, the Vermont dinner was a complete success.

I didn't know how it had happened. Maybe it was adrenaline. Maybe it was dumb luck. Maybe it was because Linda and Caroline had shown up two hours early, masked, mildly sniffly, and clearly riddled with guilt about bailing on me the week before.

"We're fine now," Caroline insisted, waving a bottle of hand sanitizer. "Mostly. Ninety percent. Ish."

Linda had brought soup and also, somehow, commandeered the appetizer station without me noticing. They "supervised," which really meant they ended up doing half the work while pretending not to, all while making passive-aggressive notes about my spice ratios.

Somehow, somewhere between mashing potatoes and yelling at the playlist for randomly switching to a sad girl acoustic cover of *Mr.*

Brightside, I stopped waiting for disaster. I wasn't hovering by the kitchen door, clutching a towel like a stress blanket.

I was topping off wine glasses, laughing too loudly, trying to keep pace with the conversations bubbling around the room. I caught myself smiling. I caught myself enjoying it.

Even Charlotte made a dramatic FaceTime entrance halfway through. She had buried herself under roughly nine layers of blankets, her hair a halo of sick-day chaos, blinking blearily at her screen.

"I'm here," she croaked. "I need a walkthrough. I want angles."

I held up my phone and spun slowly like I was shooting an *MTV Cribs* episode, and she nodded with fake seriousness.

"Okay," she said. "Acceptable. Tell Linda to save me some of that soup, or I will haunt her."

"I think she already knows, Charlotte; you've threatened her four times in the group chat."

"You've looked at that door like it owes you money."

I glanced down at the screen. "I have not."

"You have. At least three times since I've been on this call."

Caroline turned, eyes narrowing like she was about to join the inquisition. "Wait... are we waiting on someone?"

"We're not," I said quickly, maybe a little too quickly.

Charlotte snorted. "You're a terrible liar. It's charming, really."

"I was just checking the time."

"There's a clock on the wall," Caroline said, not helping.

"I wasn't looking for anyone!" I insisted, hands raised.

Charlotte lifted a brow from her blanket throne. "Mmm. So it's just a coincidence that you happened to glance at the door every time someone didn't walk in?"

I opened my mouth, but she kept going.

"Imara," she said, deeply serious, "Is your crush late to the party?"

I threw a kitchen towel at the couch, even though she wasn't physically there to catch it. "I do not have a crush."

"Oh my god," she gasped. "It *is* Noah."

"It's not!" I hissed.

Caroline's eyes widened like I had just confirmed everything she had ever suspected. "Wait! He was supposed to come tonight?"

"He said he might come," I mumbled.

Charlotte leaned in closer to the camera, smiling like a fox. "So you've been watching the door like a sad little rom-com heroine for nothing?"

"I'm not watching the door," I said, cheeks burning. "I'm— multitasking."

Caroline hummed. "Sure, babe."

"I hate everyone in this room. And also on this call."

But my eyes drifted toward the door one more time anyway.

And I pretended not to notice that Charlotte was absolutely cackling on mute.

Still no Noah.

He said he'd come.

Not that I cared. I mean, it was fine. He was probably buried under café chaos, fixing another espresso machine, alphabetizing his syrup rack, or doing whatever he did when he wasn't criticizing my carrots.

Still... I had thought he'd show.

And it bothered me that he hadn't.

It bothered me more than I noticed it bothered me.

I didn't like that.

I never would've done something like this back home. Not in my old apartment. Not with those neighbors. Not in that version of my life. But here? People had shown up. People helped.

Some had brought their friends, people I barely knew, who I had thought might feel awkward or out of place, but instead, they folded right in as if they had always belonged.

I topped off someone's cider glass when Caroline grabbed my arm and tugged me toward the kitchen, eyes gleaming like she had just won something.

"You have to meet him," she stage-whispered.

"Meet who?" I whispered back, mostly out of habit; this party wasn't exactly a monastery.

"My friend," she said, drawing out the word with too much dramatic emphasis to mean anything casual.

The "friend" in question had turned out to be tall, broad-shouldered, blue-eyed, and wearing a flannel that looked tailored-made to fit him and just him.

"Imara, this is Beau," Caroline said while giggling. "He's the one I told you about."

Beau grinned and offered a hand—warm, firm, and calloused like he probably fixed things just for fun. "It's nice to finally meet you, Imara. I've actually heard a lot about you. You're the traveling nurse who keeps everybody laughing, yeah?"

I raised a brow as I shook his hand. "I don't know about being funny," I said. "I'm mildly sarcastic at best. But it's good to know I have a reputation. It's nice to meet you as well, Beau."

Caroline nudged him with her elbow, her face fully flushed. "She downplays everything. Don't let her fool you."

Beau chuckled, glancing at her like she hung the stars. "I believe that."

Linda spotted them from across the room, one boot up on a stool as she and two locals debated whose leather was more "authentically weathered." She clocked the heart-eyes happening and fanned herself with a napkin, mouthing 'get it, girl' in my direction.

Watching them—Caroline with her heart in her eyes, Beau with that easy charm—tugged at something in me. Something small and sore and slightly bitter.

Once upon a time, someone looked at me like I had been the whole sky. And now... now I was there, holding a glass of wine and pretending my heart wasn't still recovering. But that was the thing about heartbreak: it didn't wait for the perfect moment to ruin your vibe.

So I took a deep breath, plastered on my best smile, and toasted the moment.

To friends.

To new beginnings.

To learning, slowly, that I was still whole—even without someone looking at me like I was their entire damn sky.

Because love wasn't on the radar.

Not right, then.

Maybe not ever.

The universe had a cruel sense of timing; in this instance, it was a knock at the door.

I set my glass down and walked toward the door like it was a trap. I hadn't rushed—definitely hadn't rushed. Just casually, normally, like I wasn't dying inside.

I opened it.

And—yep.

Of course.

Noah.

He was in a black shirt, his sleeves rolled up, and his curls slightly damp as if he'd just run there from something inconvenient and noble. He was holding a bottle of wine like it was a peace offering and scanning the room over my shoulder like he was looking for something or someone.

As usual, Caroline came to stand next to me, clocked him in 0.3 seconds, and let out a singsong, "Ooooh, look who finally decided to show!"

I just grabbed a deviled egg off the platter and, without breaking eye contact, shoved it into Caroline's mouth.

She squeaked and nearly choked on a laugh, her eyes wide with shock and betrayal, but she was too busy chewing to keep taunting me, which was the point.

"Well, well," he said, stepping inside like he owned the place. "Didn't realize this was a formal affair. If I'd known, I would've shaved. Or ironed something."

His eyes swept down—a quick but unmistakable pause—and I suddenly remembered my boots, the fitted jeans I had almost not worn, the orange cardigan I'd spent way too long debating because "fall-themed" felt charming and ridiculous, and the lipstick.

Ugh, the lipstick. It was a different shade than I usually wore: bolder, darker. I bought it on a whim. Now the only thing on my mind was whether it was screaming, "Please notice me."

"Is the lipstick too much?" I blurted, then instantly regretted it.

Noah blinked, tilting his head a little. "No," he said. "Not too much."

"You look..." His gaze lingered, and his smirk returned, slower this time. "Not like someone who spent the afternoon peeling potatoes."

I raised an eyebrow. "I try. The potato peelings are tucked right under my belt."

He huffed a quiet laugh, then glanced around the space, his eyes scanning the soft lighting, the mismatched but somehow perfect table setup, the buzz of conversation still going strong.

"This looks... really good," he said after a second, and it wasn't just polite. There was something genuine in it.

I cleared my throat and stepped back. "Caroline almost died from an unsolicited deviled egg, but other than that, everyone's having fun and enjoying the food. Let's call it a win."

He held up the bottle of wine. "Well, I come bearing a peace offering. I had to close late. Some guy spilled an entire iced mocha into the pastry case. The croissants did not survive."

I took the bottle with a small nod. "Tragic. For the croissants."

He followed me into the kitchen, glancing around at the mostly cleared counters and the half-drunk bottle of rosé someone had abandoned. I opened the microwave, pulled out a covered plate, and set it on the counter.

His brow lifted. "Is that for...?"

I shot him a warning look. "Don't say anything."

He held his hands up in surrender, grinning as I handed him a fork.

The first bite went in with a smirk on his face. "Wow," he said, mouth half full, "these Brussels sprouts are almost edible. I see you took my advice on the maple syrup."

I narrowed my eyes. "You can leave."

He was already taking another bite, slower this time. More thoughtfully. Then another.

He looked up, a little surprised. "Okay... all jokes aside. This is actually good. You really couldn't cook before this?"

I shrugged, trying my best to look casual as I leaned back against the counter. "I mean... here and there, I'd throw something together. Pasta. Stir fry. Basic stuff. But Vermonters? You guys go all out."

That made him laugh, a low, genuine laugh that started in his chest. "No need to be nervous," he said, nudging his plate a little closer. "You fit right in."

The words hung there, just a second too long, not in a heavy way, but just enough to make my stomach do that stupid little flip again.

I remembered the curl of his hair, slightly unruly from the wind, and the way he chewed, carefully and neatly, as if he were savoring every bite but didn't want to make a thing of it.

He wasn't even trying.

I busied myself by adjusting a nonexistent wrinkle in the table runner. "Make sure you tell Mrs. Carter that and save her a plate on your way out."

He looked up from his plate, eyebrow raised. "You trying to get rid of me already?"

He grinned down at me, a glint in his eye: playful, warm, and stupidly gorgeous.

"Rein it in, Imara," I thought.

The night smoothed out after that. Noah blended into the edges of the room, chatting with people, sipping wine, and occasionally shooting me a look across the table that I pretended not to see. Linda and Caroline, of course, noticed everything.

I caught them whispering and giggling at one point, both of them looking at me like I was a walking plot twist. I flipped them off under the table, and they blew me kisses.

Then Charlotte sent an aggressive string of texts in the group chat:

CHARLOTTE:

"Why is no one live-streaming?

Who is that man with the wine?"

IMARA:

"WHO IS THE MAN WITH THE WINE!!"

I ignored her. Mostly.

As the music softened and the laughter faded to a gentle hum, people started trickling out, grabbing coats, exchanging hugs, and sneakily claiming Tupperware.

Beau appeared at the door, ready to play chauffeur, and Caroline sighed dramatically like she was starring in a country love song. Linda hugged me tight, then leaned in to whisper, "He's cute even if he came late. And he doesn't look too eager to go either. Don't do anything I wouldn't."

I snorted, "Get in the car."

Caroline kissed my cheek. "Proud of you. And that playlist was flawless."

Beau opened the door for them with a quiet smile. I watched them disappear into the night. The door clicked shut, and I glanced over my shoulder, fully expecting Noah to be halfway out the door already.

He had shown up, brought wine, and eaten the plate I totally hadn't made specifically for him. His duty was over.

But he rolled up his sleeves as if it were some kind of silent performance and started stacking dishes without a word.

I stared at him. "No witty exit line?"

He didn't look up as he slid a plate into the sink. "Not tonight; if you stay up washing all these dishes alone, who'll help my grandmother tomorrow?"

"Wow!" I giggled, taking a sponge into my hand. "So this is about protecting your interests. Got it."

He shrugged, but there was a tiny smile playing on his lips.

We fell into a rhythm: quiet, domestic, and just the tiniest bit surreal.

I slid a wet bowl into the drying rack and reached for the last glass, which was tall, clear, with a faint pink lipstick stain that made me cringe a little.

But just as my fingers brushed the rim, so did his.

Our shoulders bumped—not a tap, but a full, firm body against body press in the cramped space between the sink and the counter. It was warm, solid, and unexpected.

"Sorry," I murmured, already stepping back and letting him take it. I forced my hand to drop to my side, even though I could still feel where he'd touched me.

He didn't flinch. He didn't rush. He just smirked, an infuriatingly slow, unreadable Noah West smirk.

Then he took the glass and dried it slowly, and I swore he was doing it with more care than was necessary. His shirt brushed my arm. His scent curled into the air—clean, warm, subtle. Something earthy and citrusy, like bergamot and cedar—and no, thank you, not tonight.

I pretended to adjust the towel on my shoulder as if that moment hadn't short-circuited my brain. I glanced up, and he was already looking at me.

We just stared at each other for a beat too long. My pulse stumbled, and my brain yelled "danger, danger" in big red flashing lights.

I cleared my throat, suddenly hyperaware of everything: how close we were standing to each other, how quiet the apartment was now, and apparently, how good he smelled without cologne.

"Hey," I said, my voice softer than I meant or would have wanted it to be. "Thanks."

He tilted his head. "For what?"

"For... I don't know. The confidence to actually do this. Your notes. That one chaotic lesson that turned into a two-hour debate about garlic."

His smirk softened into something gentler and more real. "You didn't need me. You just needed someone to tell you it wouldn't catch fire."

The silence stretched again, comfortable but charged as if the kitchen was holding its breath with me.

I shoved the dish towel into his hands and stepped back.

"Okay. Out."

He blinked. "What?"

"Out," I repeated, waving him toward the door. "You've fulfilled your dishwashing quota, and as much as I appreciate you, my bed's calling."

He chuckled but didn't argue. He just grabbed his jacket and stumbled toward the door. He paused before I could close it, giving me one last look.

"Night, Imara."

"Night."

I closed the door behind him and pressed my back against it, exhaling hard.

CHAPTER 6: PITY SOUP

It was too early for my badge to be crooked and my brain to be this foggy, but here we were. It was Monday, the most disrespectful day of the week. I was already two sips into a lukewarm coffee and internally reciting my patient list like it was my survival mantra.

George. Sally. Donald.

George checked in with chest pain that turned out to be a burrito-induced panic attack—a spicy pork combo, according to his chart. He insisted it was "a religious experience" and kept asking if he could rate our EKG machine on Yelp.

Sally was a regular. She'd sprained her ankle again while doing yoga. She had worn a shirt that said Namaste on the Farm and had a Bluetooth speaker clipped to her IV pole playing ocean sounds.

And then there was Donald, who somehow inhaled a button. Not swallowed, inhaled! His excuse was, "I was trying to hold it in my mouth while sewing." Donald, who was seventy-two, was arguing with the attending nurse about whether pudding should count as a valid breakfast food.

I looked at my chart, trying to remember who I hadn't seen yet. George was stable, Sally was probably FaceTiming her goats again, and I was still waiting on a room update for Mrs. Carter because, knowing her, she was either charming the entire staff or bullying someone into smuggling her cinnamon chai.

I stepped into the hallway, scanning the patient board to see my next heading. My hand was halfway flipping through my notes when a voice interrupted me.

"Hey."

I jolted slightly, startled.

Dr. Whitaker suddenly appeared beside me, standing as if he had teleported in from thin air. He clutched a clipboard in one hand and looked slightly more tired than usual.

"Oh—hey," I said, recovering quickly. "I didn't hear you coming."

He gave me a small, apologetic smile. "Sorry. Didn't mean to sneak up on you."

My shoulders relaxed a bit. "It's okay."

There was a beat before he added, "I'm sorry I couldn't make it Saturday."

For a second, I blinked—thrown off by the mention of the party. I smiled reflexively. "It's okay. It went well; actually, it was a success, somehow."

I felt a small pang in my chest when I said it. Not because he hadn't been there—truthfully, I hadn't even noticed—but because now that he was here saying it aloud, it felt strange to admit.

He nodded, his lips pressing together. "My dog died. Saturday morning."

"Oh," I said, softening instantly. "Sam. I'm so sorry."

His eyes flicked away for a moment, focusing on something off to the side. "It was sudden. He was thirteen. I had him since med school." His voice cracked slightly, and he quickly cleared his throat.

I hesitated, not wanting to rush him but not being quite sure what else to say. "That's a long time," I finally murmured, my hand gently touching his arm. "I'm really sorry."

He nodded again, his expression weary but appreciative. Something was there, something I couldn't read clearly, but it felt like he was about to say more. But he opened his mouth, paused, then—

The door to the hospital entrance swung open, and I heard the faint shuffle of footsteps.

My heart skipped a beat when I glanced up. Noah stepped through the doorway, effortlessly looking so Noah. He held two paper bags in his hands—the kind that crinkled when held too tight. His white t-shirt stretched over his chest, revealing a physique I had noticed before but was suddenly hyper-aware of at that moment.

When his eyes met mine across the hallway, the smile that lit up his face made it feel like someone had turned the heat up in the room.

I held his gaze a second too long, and suddenly everything else faded. Sam's voice became muffled as if he were speaking underwater.

I heard Noah's footsteps, soft against the hospital floor, and before I could think to blink, he was standing just a few feet away from me.

"Good afternoon," he said politely, giving Sam a small nod as he approached. Sam turned, clearly caught mid-thought, his expression edging into confusion.

"Brought lunch for Ma," Noah said, holding up one of the bags casually. Then, without skipping a beat, he extended the second bag in my direction. "And for you."

I blinked. "What's this?"

He shrugged. "I felt like it would've been rude not to." My heart stuttered. It wasn't a grand gesture, but it was something. And he said it so simply as if he'd thought of me—like it were obvious.

I opened the top of the container and glanced inside. Soup. Of course.

But his eyes remained on mine, lingering just a little too long.

I narrowed my gaze in return. "So this was pity soup?"

Noah huffed a quiet laugh and shook his head. "I figured you were tired of eating leftovers."

I couldn't bring myself to say anything. I felt the warmth of the bowl through the bag and became acutely aware of the space between us.

Beside me, Sam cleared his throat.

I glanced over. He was watching the exchange with a faint crease between his brows—not angry, not even annoyed—just trying to piece something together. There was a flicker of surprise on his face, or perhaps something quieter, like realization.

While there was nothing technically wrong with receiving soup from a patient's grandson, there was also no way to make it not look a little personal.

There was nothing to explain because there was nothing to explain.

Still, I lifted the bowl and, with a lightness I didn't quite feel, said, "I'm not above accepting bribes, you know."

Sam chuckled faintly, but the sound didn't stick. He lingered for a moment as if he wanted to say something else, but he didn't. Instead, he nodded and turned, walking down the corridor.

Noah was quiet for a beat, watching after him, the corners of his mouth tugging upward as if he were halfway to a smirk but not in a hurry to land one.

"What?"

"Bribes, huh?"

I rolled my eyes, turning back toward my computer. "Thank you for the soup, mister. Go check on your grandmother. I have actual work to do."

His gaze softened just a little, and neither of us said anything for a second. He nodded once. "You're welcome."

With that, he disappeared down the hallway, leaving behind a bowl of something warm, a quiet storm in my chest, and far too many thoughts I hadn't had time for.

Later, my phone buzzed with a flurry of messages in our group chat:

Me: Should I even be here?

Me: This is stupid, right?

Charlotte: WHAT

Caroline: GIRL, GO IN

Linda: Are you texting us from the sidewalk?

Charlotte: You came all this way. Thank him for the soup again!

Caroline: Also, maybe flirt a little? Just saying.

Me: I won't be doing that.

Linda: Just go in. You know you want to.

Charlotte: You're not leaving without a cookie, so stop pretending this is about manners.

I glanced up from the screen and at the cute little sign that read "Noah's Sweet Escape." I wondered what I was doing here, Imara. You had just seen him at the hospital. Except that was five hours ago, and now this was different. Besides, I was just passing by: what if I wanted coffee to go?

I pushed open the door before I could spiral further. The bell chimed again, soft and cheerful, and the warmth hit me like a wave: coffee, sugar, spice, something citrusy I couldn't quite place. It was almost enough to make me forget why I was hesitating in the first place. Almost.

Noah looked up from behind the counter, mid-conversation with the cashier. He said something too quietly for me to hear, then turned his head and saw me. His lips curled into a smile—a knowing look in his eyes—and I had to hide my blush beneath my scarf.

There was a flicker of surprise—just a flicker—but it wasn't the bad kind. He did not look displeased; he just looked like I'd caught him off guard in that still-waking-up way of his.

"I didn't think I'd see you again so soon," he said once the register dinged shut. "How's the soup holding up?"

I arched a brow. "Disappointingly good. Kind of ruined my plan to slander your culinary skills publicly."

He smirked. "Tragic."

He gestured to the espresso machine while still watching me. "Well, since you're here... the usual?"

I hesitated for a second. "And maybe a cookie."

He raised a brow, pretending to be scandalized. "Look at you, breaking patterns." Then, to his cashier, he said, "Taking five." The poor girl nearly dropped a stack of sleeves, her eyes wide as she stared at her boss's retreating—and then at me. "Uh—yeah, sure. Totally."

He nodded toward the window. "Weather bothering you yet?"

"A little," I admitted, blowing into the cup. "I thought I had seen bad winters before, but this cold was something else. I wasn't even driving to work anymore."

His expression tightened just a little. "You were walking?"

I nodded, wrapping both hands around the cup. "It felt safer than skidding off the road. Besides, my step count had never been better."

He didn't laugh; he frowned. "If you need a ride, just ask. Vermont is quiet, but it's largely harmless."

I raised an eyebrow. "You almost sounded concerned."

His eyes rolled. "My grandmother would kill me if something happened to you."

A small silence settled between us. I gave him a small smile, a little amused. "So that was the only reason?"

There was a pause—barely a beat—but it was there. Noah glanced at me, then back out the window. "It was a good enough reason. Why? Were you hoping it would have been something else?"

I choked on my sip—enough that I coughed once, set the cup down a little too fast, and immediately reached for a napkin as if it were going to save me from the heat suddenly blooming in my cheeks. My eyes darted everywhere—the window, the cup, the floor, the ceiling— but on Noah as I tucked a twist of hair behind my ear.

"No, no, just... just curious."

I cleared my throat and went back to sipping my coffee. We sat in a silence that wasn't awkward, just full as if neither of us was eager to break it. I could feel him watching me. Not smug, not teasing—just quietly entertained.

Outside, the snow kept falling in lazy spirals, and inside, everything felt too still for just two people and a cup of coffee.

He shifted in his seat, stretching back with that same quiet presence he always carried. "I used to hate winter," he said, his eyes on the snow. "Too quiet. Too slow. Made it easy to think."

I glanced at him. "Think about...?"

He hesitated, then gave me a small shrug. "The stuff you avoided when the days moved faster."

"Very... insightful, thank you for that."

He smirked without looking at me. "I tried."

"I was looking at your walls earlier," I said, nodding toward the front of the café. "The photos. The music. The little touches."

His attention returned to me, and I could tell I had surprised him.

"It felt intentional," I continued. "Like you had carved out something personal. Especially here, in Vermont."

He smiled just a little. "I guess I did."

"It made me feel good," I admitted, not exactly sure where I was going with this conversation. "Walking into a space and seeing your culture reflected at you. The art, the records, and even the way the place smelled like cinnamon and brown sugar instead of bleach and burnt espresso."

That made him laugh, a quiet and low rumbling from his chest as he patted it.

"I wasn't sure how it would go over," he admitted. "Taking over a place like this, in a state that doesn't exactly scream diversity."

"But you did it anyway."

He nodded. "I didn't see the point in building something I didn't recognize."

I drained the last of my coffee and held the empty cup between my palms longer than I needed to. The warmth had faded, but I pretended otherwise. Something about that moment—the stillness, the gentle snow, the easy way he talked—made me want to linger.

Noah glanced outside again, his brow faintly creased. "It's really coming down now."

I followed his gaze. The sidewalk had disappeared under a layer of white, and the streetlights were fuzzy around the edges as if they were spiraling in a snow globe.

He looked back at me.

"I'll walk you," he said.

I shook my head too quickly. "No, it's fine. I'm good."

He gave me a mildly skeptical look. "You sure? It's getting ugly out there."

The thing was—I wanted to say yes. I really wanted to say yes. I longed to let Noah walk me home and let the wind tangle my hair while he walked close enough to block it—to let myself feel cared for. But that was dangerous territory, and I wasn't stupid.

I smiled. "Someone's gotta hold down the fort, right? If you abandon this place, who will fix your espresso machine when it has another meltdown?"

I stood and tugged on my gloves. "Thanks for the coffee."

His voice was lower when he replied. "Anytime."

I pushed the door open and stepped out into the cold; the wind hit my face like a reminder. Snow had already piled in the sidewalk creases, but I didn't stop walking.

I vowed not to look back.

I absolutely would not—

Okay, fine. I took one glance.

He was still at the window, watching.

I tugged my scarf up over my mouth, my cheeks burning from more than just the cold.

It was fine. It was all completely fine.

I was just cold and maybe smiling. A little.

That's all.

CHAPTER 7: DECEPTIVELY BEAUTIFUL

I didn't know who had given Charlotte and Caroline this much power, but I filed an emotional restraining order. Somehow, they'd roped me into a group sledding trip. Yes. Sledding.

I was literally throwing myself down a snowy hill on a glorified plastic plate like a snow globe extra. Apparently, this was peak Vermont living. "Character building," Charlotte had said with a perfectly straight face, even though she was still recovering from a brutal flu that had kept her out of work for half a week.

Somehow, despite all of us being on rotating shifts at the hospital, we were all off that day—a rare Sunday miracle. I wouldn't have been surprised if Charlotte orchestrated the whole thing from her bed, with a tissue box in one hand and schedule requests in the other.

Linda, on the other hand, wasn't there. Her father was still recovering back home; the last I heard, she had flown out on Friday to be with him for a few days. I hoped she was warm. I hoped she was safe. I hoped she wasn't, at that very moment, about to hurl herself down a mountain in a puffer coat.

"You'll love it," Caroline beamed as we stepped out of the car once we were at the mountain resort.

I squinted at the scene in front of me like it was a foreign planet, which, frankly, it might as well have been. The resort was at the edge of a thick, snow-draped forest, its peaked rooftops dusted with white.

A lodge stood in the center, its woodsmoke curling from the chimney. Children darted around like caffeinated marshmallows, their parents trailing behind, and somewhere off to the left, a group of teenagers were already launching themselves down the slope with wild, feral joy. It was loud and chaotic. And absolutely none of it felt beginner-friendly.

Caroline was already halfway across the parking lot, stomping through the snow in her oversized boots as if she were born for this. Her hat was a giant pom-pom monstrosity, and she was drinking her hot cocoa with the enthusiasm of a winter soldier.

Meanwhile, I was still adjusting my scarf and wondering how I had let myself be peer-pressured into what was clearly the start of a cautionary tale. I shuffled after everyone, half-bundled in borrowed snow gear that faintly smelled of pine and detergent, feeling like a fraud.

Sledding? Down a mountain?

Yeah. No. Absolutely not.

"Can't I just watch from the sidelines?" I ask hopefully. "Provide moral support? Cheer you on while staying alive?"

"Nope," Caroline said.

Charlotte handed me a sled. "Welcome to Vermont, baby."

I stared at it.

It stared back.

We were not friends.

Before I could fully mentally prepare myself to die by sled, a new set of footsteps crunched through the snow behind us. I turned, already squinting against the glare, then froze.

He was tall, bundled in a navy jacket and knit beanie, his hair peeking out and cheeks flushed from the cold or the walk. His jaw looked slightly clenched as if he was questioning every decision that had led him to that precise moment. And his eyes landed on me and didn't budge.

"Noah? What... are you doing here?" I asked, trying to keep my tone casual but failing miserably at it.

He opened his mouth, eyebrows knitted together, but Charlotte swooped in, her voice pitched just high enough to be suspiciously innocent. She threw her arms over my shoulder, "Oh, right. We forgot to tell you!"

I narrowed my eyes.

"That we invited Noah!" Caroline added, glancing at Charlotte, who offered a sheepish thumbs-up and a "What, he's fun!" shrug.

Noah visibly blanched. "Wait—she didn't know?"

He looked at me again; guilt stamped across his face as if he was already preparing to bolt back to from where he'd come.

"I can leave," Noah said quickly, lifting both hands like he was easing away from a crime scene. "Linda told me you knew. You probably just forgot to ask because you've been so busy lately. But it's fine—I should probably go prep for tomorrow anyway—"

"It's fine," I cut in, sharper than I meant to.

Everyone stopped.

I cleared my throat, adjusting my scarf as if it were going to hide the fact that my face was officially on fire. "Seriously. You can stay. We're all already geared up."

Charlotte and Caroline immediately burst into a synchronized chorus of "Yay!" as if we had reached the third act of a rom-com, and I was the adorably clueless lead in desperate need of meddling.

It was so wildly out of character for Charlotte that I whipped my head around and eyed her suspiciously.

Noah just watched me. He was still uncertain; I could see it the way he held his gear, but at least now he was smiling a little.

The hill was deceptively beautiful, a soft, rolling slope dusted with fresh powder framed by pine trees that looked imported from a postcard. But don't let it fool you—this hill was a liar—a trap.

My first run ended in disaster.

I barely managed to sit before the sled tipped awkwardly to the side, launching me into motion, and I immediately spun sideways like a rogue curling stone. I shrieked the whole way down, arms flailing, my scarf whipping in the wind, until I toppled over into a snowbank with all the grace of a dropped grocery bag.

I lay there briefly, blinking at the pale sky, wondering if it was too early to fake a sprained ankle.

Caroline doubled over at the bottom of the hill, red-faced and howling with laughter, one mittened hand slapping her knee. "I can't breathe," she wheezed. "You looked like a flying raccoon!"

The next time I tried, Charlotte yelled, "LEAN BACK BUT NOT TOO FAR! THINK LIKE A—"

I groaned and hauled myself up, with snow clinging to my coat like regret. The sled dragged behind me like a sulking child as I trudged back up the hill for another go.

I tried again and again.

On the fourth time, I nearly took out a very startled child.

Each time I caught Noah from the corner of my eye, he was leaning casually against a wooden fence post at the base of the hill, with his hands tucked into his jacket pockets and his knit cap pulled low over his curls. His breath clouded in the cold as he watched me with that familiar, maddening smirk tugging at his mouth every time I ate snow.

I stomped past him again, dragging the sled behind me as if it had insulted my ancestors.

"I don't want to hear you," I huffed, half-breathless, half-snow-drenched, glaring as I leaned against the fence beside him.

He chuckled, low and warm. "You don't even want a little encouragement?"

Another glare. I was perfecting the art.

He didn't move at first; he just tilted his head, his gaze skimming over me in a way that always felt like it saw more than it should. Then he softly and casually reached out and brushed something off my hair. Ice crystals, probably. But the way his gloved fingers swept along the edge of my pixie cut made my breath snag.

We locked eyes. Just for a second. Maybe less.

His lips parted slightly, but before he could say anything, he cleared his throat and stepped back.

"I'm gonna give it a try," he said, his voice rougher than before as he bent to grab the spare sled.

And, of course, he did amazing, almost as if he had been doing it since childhood. He was graceful and composed, not a single wild flail in sight. When he reached the bottom, he spun into a slow stop and looked back up as if waiting for his score.

Show-off.

I groaned, adjusted my gloves, and picked up the sled again.

Fine. One more run.

I heard Noah's clear and confident voice from the top of the hill: "Weight to the right! There you go! Just like that!"

The sled glided smoother this time, the kind of smooth that made you feel like you'd finally figured something out. The wind kissed my face, and my cheeks stung from the cold, but I was laughing— real, unfiltered laughter—because I was doing it. I was flying.

I loosened my grip just a little and let the hill carry me.

The world was bright and sharp and alive until it wasn't.

I didn't see the rut—a rough patch of churned-up snow—because it blended too easily into the slope. But the moment I hit it, everything jerked.

The sled bucked beneath me like a wild thing. My balance shattered.

My legs lifted, my stomach dropped, and for a split second, there was nothing but sky, snow, and the sickening feeling of something going wrong.

The world tilted before the ground rushed up and slammed into me with brutal force. My shoulder hit first, then my side, then my knee. I uncontrollably tumbled through ice-packed powder, the cold slicing through my clothes like broken glass.

A cry tore from my throat, but the snow swallowed it. The world muffled. All sound turned distant as if I had slipped underwater. I landed facedown, half-buried and breathless.

A sharp and immediate pain bloomed, and a white-hot and relentless shock shock rolled through me.

The fall punched the wind out of my lungs. I gasped once, then twice, but no air came in. My mouth opened, but nothing filled it. The sky above me blurred, spinning, and a single tear slid from the corner of my eye before freezing on my cheek.

Panic took root in my chest.

I tried to speak or cry out, but the snow pressed in, cold and quiet, muffling the edges of my thoughts.

"Noah," I thought, or maybe whispered—or maybe not at all.

Then,

"No, no—hey, hey, I got you."

His voice broke through the fog like sunlight cracking ice.

He was there in a flash, crouched low beside me, breath coming fast, his curls damp with snow, eyes wide and searching. One gloved hand braced my shoulder, and the other hovered as if touching me might make it worse.

"Are you hurt?" His voice was low, urgent. "Imara, talk to me. Where does it hurt?"

I inhaled, finally, and let out a long, shaky breath.

"I... I think I'm okay."

His brow furrowed.

I shifted slightly, then winced, the pain catching low in my side, dull.

"Mild pain. Nothing broken. I think the ice just... I don't know, absorbed it."

He didn't laugh. Instead, he gently, methodically started checking me over. His touch was careful—deliberate but soft—as if he were afraid I might crack.

I should have said something, perhaps even made a joke or brushed it off. But I didn't.

I just let him tug my glove off to check my wrist and ease his hand beneath my coat to press lightly against my ribs.

My eyes quickly flicked away to the trees, the snow, and everywhere but his face. But it was too late: my cheeks were already warming beneath the sting of the cold, flushed in a way that had nothing to do with the fall.

His hand stayed there, steady against my side. His head ducked slightly, brows furrowed in quiet focus.

I bit the inside of my cheek hard because I shouldn't have been thinking about how good he smelled, how his skin felt through his gloves, or how every inch of me buzzed with a hundred little sensations. I had absolutely no business feeling right then.

I was warm everywhere he touched—even with layers between us.

He glanced up, meeting my eyes.

"You sure nothing's broken?"

"Pretty sure," I whispered.

He nodded once, and that was it: he didn't press further. He just helped me sit up slowly, his hand still braced at the small of my back.

"That one scared me."

"I know," he said.

I could see it written across his face, in the way he wasn't letting go yet and how his brow furrowed as he watched me breathe.

I glanced up at him.

We were so close. Closer than we had ever been without all the noise between us. We just sat there in the snow: I was rattled and trying to pretend I was fine, and Noah was holding me as if he was not going anywhere until he was sure I also believed it.

I was relieved no one else saw.

"I'm over it," I said, forcing a shaky laugh. "Get me out of this suit before I overheat and die dramatically in the snow."

My voice slightly wobbled at the end, but I hoped the chuckle covered it. Noah helped me to my feet with that same quiet gentleness that made it hard to meet his eyes.

I shook off the nerves—or pretended to.

By the time we reached the top of the hill again, the others were still moving around, clearly not too bothered that I had disappeared with Noah. Charlotte held out a thermos.

"You alive?"

"Barely," I muttered, taking the cocoa with a wink meant to be playful, even though my ribs still ached and I was definitely walking like someone twice my age.

Caroline and Charlotte returned to shrieking with laughter, sleds flying, limbs flailing like the chaos agents they were.

"Let's just leave them be," Noah said, and I nodded, already turning away.

Eventually, we ended up near the artificial cocoa pit the resort had set up—an oversized fire table surrounded by benches and snow-damp towels. The steam from my cup curled up into the cold air as I sat, still bundled in half-unzipped gear and bruised pride.

He dropped onto the bench beside me, a little stiff—quiet in a way that didn't feel uncomfortable anymore.

I glanced over at him.

"How are you so good at sledding? Have you secretly trained for this your whole life?"

He smirked, eyes flicking sideways.

"Came with the Vermont starter pack. Right after flannel and maple syrup snobbery. It was either learn how to fall without breaking something or stay inside alone."

I laughed softly as I sipped my cocoa, but something in his tone tugged at me. I glanced sideways, past the steam rising from my cup.

His leg bounced lightly, an unconscious rhythm against the packed snow beneath the bench. His eyes kept flicking to his phone screen, then back again. His fingers toyed with the sleeve of his glove, and restlessness leaked out of him in small, constant movements.

He didn't know how to be still. Not really.

I recognized it because I had spent months doing the same thing: filling the quiet with lists, distractions, and motion while pretending that being busy meant I was okay. Pretending it was healing when it was just hiding.

"Why'd you come?"

He glanced up from his cocoa.

"What do you mean?"

"I mean," I said, tilting my head, "you've got a café to run. And yet... here you are. Spending your Sunday getting snow in places no human being should."

Noah was quiet for a beat.

"I don't know," he said finally. He exhaled through his nose, his gaze dropping to his hands. "Guess I'm just tired of smelling butter and flour all the time. My other senses were feeling neglected."

"You really don't talk that much, you know?" I said, half smiling. "All your answers seem so... well put together. Like you've had time to rehearse."

He huffed a quiet laugh, one corner of his mouth twitching upward. He didn't look at me right away; he just kept his eyes on the cocoa in his hands, steam rising between his fingers like smoke from a vibrant memory.

"I don't like saying things I can't take back," he said after a moment. "So I think first, and now it's subconsciously applied to everything I say. Doesn't always help, but it slows me down."

I tilted my head, watching him from over the rim of my cup.

"That sounds... exhausting."

His eyes finally lifted, meeting mine.

"Sometimes it is."

His jaw tightened as if he were about to swallow the next sentence, but he didn't. Then, almost as if he blurted it just to get it over with, he said, "You know, my grandmother has a habit of doing that. Taking people in."

I glanced at him.

"You mean...?"

His eyes stayed on the fire pit as if the rising steam made it easier to keep talking.

"I was five when she brought me home. Technically, it was my mom who did all the paperwork. But Grandma made it feel like I wasn't just filling a spare room."

My heart caught a little.

He said it so matter-of-factly, but there was something in how his voice dipped.

"She's tough," I said softly. "But she loves you."

"I know," he replied. "It's just... weird. Even now, the love she gives feels strange. I spent so long pretending I didn't care what people thought and didn't need anyone; she slapped those feelings right out of me when she started nurturing me. But lately, I feel like I'm always halfway in a room, just waiting to figure out if I belong there."

I felt that so deeply it sat heavily on my chest, curling around my ribs as if it had lived there all along. I had spent months trying to find where I fit—what I was supposed to be doing, how not to mess it up, how not to let anyone down, and whether I was good enough. Whether I was... enough, period.

I opened my mouth to say something but closed it again and looked down at my cup.

"I get that."

He glanced over, his gaze searching.

"Yeah?"

"Yeah," I said, not quite ready to explain why. "Let's just say Vermont's quieter than I thought but loud in all the ways I didn't expect."

He smiled at that.

"I know exactly what you mean."

I swore it made my chest ache just a little. The fire crackled. The others were still yelling and laughing up the hill, but their voices felt muffled now—like they were miles away.

It was just the two of us there.

I was still sore from the fall, and he was still hiding things behind that easy calm.

I blew gently across my cocoa, trying to focus on anything but the warmth blooming somewhere inside me that had nothing to do with the drink.

CHAPTER 8: GOLDEN MINI PIES

After hours of fluorescent lights, rushed charting, and half-eaten granola bars that wished they were dinner, I often ended up at Noah's café more often than I wanted to admit.

I hadn't planned it. It wasn't that obvious. At least, I hoped I wasn't. But somehow, my boots kept steering me in that direction, like muscle memory, magnetic pull, or whatever excuse I pretended not to analyze too deeply that night.

It was close to six, just dark enough for the sky to press in around the streetlights and for the wind to sting my cheeks as I crunched across the salted sidewalk. I had shoved my gloves halfway into my pockets, my scarf tugged loose, and my tiredness felt less heavy knowing where I was going. I hummed a little under my breath—off-key but content. And honestly, that was somewhat new for me.

The door closed behind me with a soft chime, leaving the cold outside as warmth wrapped around me like it knew I needed it.

Noah was at the counter, wiping it down like he did every night around that time. He glanced up before the bell above the door could take a bow after chiming, already reaching for a mug.

"Evening," he said as if it was routine now—as if we did this every day.

I shook the snow from my coat and tugged my scarf loose as I made my way to the counter. "You always look surprised to see me," I remarked.

"You can't blame me. Can you? A gorgeous woman like yourself stopping by after a long shift. Sometimes I wonder what I did right," he replied.

I froze mid-step, my scarf still looped in one hand, snow melting in my hair, and my boots squeaking against the tile.

Did he just...?

I cleared my throat and tugged my scarf a little tighter as if it might hide the full-body blush rapidly rushing up my neck. "That's a new line," I managed, aiming for casual and landing somewhere around breathless.

He didn't even blink. Instead, he leaned over the counter and placed a small plate in front of me with the same easy confidence that scrambled every one of my neurons.

"New dessert," he said as if he hadn't just derailed my internal monologue with a single sentence. "I'm testing it out. You're getting the first taste, but don't get cocky."

I glanced down at the plate. It held something rich and glossy, with dark chocolate shavings on top and a dusting of powdered sugar like fresh snow. It was warm, still, just out of the oven—maybe.

I tried to ignore how shaky my hands felt as I reached for the fork. Not even Derek had ever made me this nervous.

I took the tiniest bite, more for survival than for evaluation. The fork pressed through a soft, buttery crust into something molten underneath—dark chocolate, warm berries, maybe orange zest? I wasn't sure because the second it hit my tongue, I stopped thinking entirely.

I blinked. Then blinked again.

Noah watched me with one eyebrow raised as if waiting for praise or curse words.

"Well?" he asked, a little nervously.

I set the fork down slowly, swallowed, and stared at him. "Okay. That's... rude."

"Rude?" he echoed.

"Yeah," I said, pointing to the plate as though it had personally offended me. "Because now I'm going to think about this every day. I'll probably start craving this in the middle of a twelve-hour shift while dealing with someone's broken hip and three family members asking about pudding. I'll start putting on weight because now I'll keep craving pies—and pudding."

His mouth curved, pleased. "So it's good."

"No, it's criminal," I said, picking the fork up again. "You should be arrested immediately."

He chuckled as he turned to the counter behind him and opened a small box tucked just out of sight.

"Also," he said casually, "these were about to disappear."

I blinked as he slid the box toward me. Inside were three perfectly golden mini pies, neatly arranged as if they were waiting for me all day.

My chest squeezed a little.

"You saved these?" I asked, my voice coming out softer than I had intended.

He shrugged, looking far too nonchalant. "People were eyeing them. I intervened."

I stared at the pies for a beat too long, a warmth that had nothing to do with sugar or cinnamon or the radiator humming in the background blooming in my chest. I tucked a curl behind my ear and smiled—a small and helpless smile that betrayed the fondness behind it.

"You're gonna ruin me! You know that, right?" I murmured.

And I should have left. I really should have.

I'd tried not to stay long when I came here. It was a little personal rule I'd made up somewhere between pie number two, and that first moment I realized the way he looked at me lingered in my chest longer than it should. Every visit made me want to stay longer, talk more, ask real questions, peel back layers, see, notice more, and admire more.

He was tall in a way that made most rooms feel smaller when he stepped in; his broad shoulders had a quiet strength that never felt forced. His smooth, rich brown skin always seemed to catch the café lights just right, and his jaw was clean-shaven that day, framed by the hair peeking out from under his cap.

There was something about the way he carried himself. It wasn't just how he looked; it was how gracefully he moved behind the counter, handled things without fuss, and how he made the quiet easier to sit in. And I was one soft word and one slow smile away from setting myself up for something I wasn't entirely sure I could afford.

So I gathered my things, trying to be subtle about how much I didn't want to get up and leave. Noah was still behind the counter, working on restocking something, but I knew he noticed the shift. His movements slowed. He glanced at the clock, then at the door.

At that moment, the wind hit, howling against the windows like it was angry, rattling the glass so hard that the open sign fluttered and fell sideways with a sad little thunk. Noah straightened, his eyebrows raised. "That didn't sound like just wind."

I walked over to the front window and pressed my fingers to the cold glass. The snow wasn't falling anymore—it was pouring. Thick, sideways sheets of it were already burying the sidewalk.

"I probably... shouldn't have waited to be the last person here," I murmured.

He joined me, arms crossed, squinting through the whiteout. "Yeah. That's not a passing storm."

It was settling in. And I was, officially, stuck.

"Well," he said, rubbing the back of his neck as if he were thinking through a plan, "it looks like you're not going anywhere for a bit."

"Yeah," I muttered, still watching the snow hammer the glass. "Totally casual. Definitely not about—" He glanced at the back kitchen before I could say anything else. "I've got ingredients. If I'm going to be stuck here playing host to a very picky guest, I might as well make dinner." I blinked. "Hey, who said I was picky?"

He looked over his shoulder, already heading toward the swinging doors. "You did. Indirectly. Every time you insulted my coffee or questioned the ratio of filling to crust in my pies."

I followed him in with a dramatic sigh. "That's called having standards."

The kitchen was warm—warmer than the front—with soft light and gleaming metal, shelves full of spices, and baskets of produce that made it feel more like a home kitchen than a business. Noah started pulling open drawers, laying ingredients across the counter like a puzzle.

"Okay," he muttered, half to himself. "We've got pasta. We've got garlic. Tomatoes. One sad-looking zucchini that might be okay if we cooked it fast..."

I picked it up and squinted. "That zucchini has seen things."

He chuckled. "You're not wrong. All right, Chef. What are we making?"

I raised an eyebrow. "We?"

His eyes met mine, steady and amused. "Unless you were planning to just supervise again."

"I was, actually."

He chuckled softly and tossed the garlic into the pan, the sizzle breaking the moment just enough before he said, "So... Virginia. What was life like before Vermont?"

I hummed, rocking on my heels. "Busy, honestly. Really busy. I was always doing something: double shifts, weekend rotations, helping my parents with errands, groceries, everything in between."

He kept stirring, but I saw his attention shift slightly toward me.

"It wasn't bad," I added quickly, "just... nonstop. There wasn't a lot of space to breathe, let alone hang out in someone's café kitchen, pretending I knew the difference between oregano and thyme."

He chuckled at that, and it made something ease in my chest.

"Anyone you left behind?"

There it was—the question everyone in this town seemed contractually obligated to ask. I sighed and pressed my fingertips to the edge of the counter.

"Why does everyone here ask that question like it's a requirement to have some big, dramatic backstory?"

He shrugged without looking at me. "Small towns like their stories. Makes it easier to place people."

"Yeah, well. Mine wasn't exactly uplifting."

His hands slowed ever so slightly, but he didn't say anything; he just waited, letting me decide if I wanted to fill the quiet. I did. Maybe because his silence wasn't demanding; it was just open.

"I was with someone," I said, my voice a little flatter than intended.

"Derek. We were together for a while. I supported him through school—med school, of all things. I even paid rent on an apartment he insisted we needed, like we were already living the life we were working for."

Noah stopped stirring and set the spoon down gently. "He said once he finished, things would change, and he'd take care of me for once. I believed him."

I swallowed, my fingers curling against the counter's edge. "But while I was working double shifts to keep us afloat... he was sleeping with my best friend."

He stopped stirring; the spoon clinked gently as he set it down. His jaw tightened, and slowly, one hand rose to his hip while the other raked through his hair, frustration bleeding through the movement.

I didn't tell Noah about the rest. About how the miscarriage had shattered me. I didn't say how long it took to admit to myself that I wasn't just heartbroken; I was wrecked.

"So while you were killing yourself to keep things going... he was sleeping with your best friend?"

I shrugged, playing it off with a weak smile. "He's her problem now."

"Imara," he said, using my name as if it mattered, as if he wanted me to hear it clearly. "I don't care how long ago it was—that man didn't just let you down. He failed you. Full stop."

His hand brushed against mine—barely a touch, just enough for every nerve ending in my body to feel it. Just enough to ground me.

"I don't know what kind of idiot throws away someone who would carry all that weight for them," he said, softer now. "But I do know it wasn't your fault. And I really hope you'd stopped carrying that like it was."

My throat tightened, and I didn't know what to say. So I nodded once, still holding his hand while trying to catch my breath in a kitchen that suddenly felt warmer than before.

A low tug that had nothing to do with the cold or the pasta and everything to do with him had formed in my stomach. He slowly let my hand go, and I could feel the warmth of his palm fading, leaving my skin a little too aware and a little too empty.

He breathed in deeply and turned back to the stove, lifting the spoon. I looked away quickly—back to the pot, back to the steam, back to pretending I hadn't just almost melted over a man stirring tomato sauce like it was therapy.

"I never really knew my birth parents," he said, drying his hands slowly. "The woman who adopted me... she didn't have a partner. No husband. Just her. She gave me her name. Raised me alone until she couldn't."

His eyes didn't lift; they just stayed trained on the sauce simmering low between us.

"She was kind. Gentle. But it was my grandmother who taught me what staying looked like. What love felt like when it wasn't trying to be perfect. Just... real."

I said nothing, but something in my chest loosened—like a door creaking open.

"When my mom passed, I thought I'd already lost everything. But grief doesn't keep score. It just... finds new ways to take. And now, watching my grandmother slow down, pretending she's fine... I know what's coming. I know what it'll cost."

He paused, his breath catching on the edge of the truth.

"That's why I don't go chasing things that'll hurt to lose—if I can help it."

It landed harder than he knew because I had spent years doing the opposite: giving, staying, breaking, and hoping something would last.

Before I could speak or ask what he was really trying to say, he set a plate in front of me, a soft smile tugging at the corner of his mouth.

"Try that before I change my mind and keep it for myself."

And just like that, we were back to dinner.

We ended up eating in the kitchen: not at a table, not across from each other, just next to each other, leaning over the counter like it was some shared ritual we'd always had. The lights were dim back there, too; our plates clinked quietly against the counter as we ate.

We fell into a rhythm that felt so natural it was a bit scary—the way we leaned closer when we spoke, how our arms kept brushing, but neither of us pulled away, and even how I kept forgetting there was a storm outside.

I set my fork down, brushing my hands on a napkin. "Alright," I said, trying to sound casual even though my heart was already too soft for that. "Next time, I cook."

Noah lifted a brow, intrigued. "Yeah?"

"Mhm." I turned to rinse our plates, feeling braver with my back turned. "Only for you, though. After a long day of juggling orders and pretending not to be impressed by me, I figured you should come home and let someone else free your hands for once."

He chuckled, low and surprised, stepping closer to set his plate beside mine. "Come home, huh?" he said slowly as if he were turning the phrase over. "You inviting me over after hours, Imara? Just the two of us?"

I glanced at him from over my shoulder, trying not to grin. "Don't read into it."

"Oh, I'm reading," he murmured, that spark of something reappearing in his eyes. "Just want to make sure I brought dessert."

My face burned so hot I almost forgot about the cold air waiting outside—and still, I didn't correct him.

CHAPTER 9: SKELETONS

"So," Caroline said, dragging the word out as if she was revving up for something dangerous. "You and Noah..."

I didn't even look up from the chart in my hand. "Don't."

"What?" she asked, all innocence and no shame. "I'm just asking."

"You're fishing."

"I'm curious," she corrected.

Before I could respond, Linda rounded the corner with a coffee in one hand and that mischievous glint in her eye. "Are we talking about Imara's boyfriend?"

"He's not my boyfriend," I replied flatly, flipping the page.

Caroline gasped—like I had just declared I hated puppies. "Wow. Just like that? You're denying his entire existence?"

"I'm denying you access to my personal life."

Linda settled against the nurse's station beside me. "We're just saying... the vibes? They've evolved."

"Strong mutual attraction energy," Caroline added, pointing her pen at me like it was a concrete piece of evidence—Exhibit A.

I snorted. "You two get one snowstorm and a shared plate of pasta, and suddenly, I'm starring in a Hallmark movie."

They nodded in unison. Rude.

"Okay, first of all, we're friends," I said, tapping the chart more forcefully than necessary. "That's it. He's nice. I'm nice. We're friendly. That's allowed."

Caroline arched a brow. "So when he looks at you like you're made of caramel and warm pastries, that's just... respectful customer service?"

"Yes," I deadpanned. "Hospitality. It's literally his job."

Linda hummed into her coffee. "He brings you food. Often. Like, scheduled often."

"He makes extras. I work long shifts. It's practical. Efficiency."

Look, yes—we spent time together. More than I had planned to. Yes, I knew his schedule, how he took his coffee, and that he always double-checked the lock even when it was already secure. Yes, he was warm in that quiet, steady way that made me forget I used to flinch when people got too close.

But Noah was busy. Focused. A man who had exactly enough room in his life for what he chose to make room for. And I was not delusional enough to believe I was that exception.

He'd never crossed a line or pushed past friendship. He never made a move, not even in the stillness of a snowstorm or the quiet after we shared a meal that felt a little too much like home.

He was my friend.

At best.

Anything else?

Wishful thinking.

Linda nudged me with her elbow. "It's okay. We're rooting for you. And honestly, if a man fed me like that every week, I'd be writing my vows in a Google Doc."

I shook my head but couldn't stop the small smile tugging at my lips.

Before Caroline could double down, Linda softened a little. "By the way, thanks for asking about my dad last week. We got some news: he's actually doing better. Stable. For the first time in months, I felt like we could exhale."

I reached over, squeezing her hand gently. "That's amazing. Seriously. I'd been thinking about you guys."

She nodded, her eyes a little glassy but smiling. "Me too. I think that might have been the turn we'd been praying for."

Caroline sighed. "Okay, emotional moment logged. Now, back to Imara and her baked goods situationship."

I groaned and shoved the chart into my bag. "I'm clocking out. You two are exhausting."

I opened my mouth to shut it all down again, but before I could deliver my dramatic exit line, a voice cut through the noise behind me.

"Imara. Can I talk to you for a moment?"

I turned, and my smile slipped, replaced by confusion.

Dr. Whitaker stood a few feet away, his hands in the pockets of his white coat, his posture unreadable. It was weeks since I turned him down, and since then, we had operated on a firm foundation of polite nods and strategic eye contact—just enough to keep things from tipping into awkward territory.

Now, though, he was looking directly at me.

Caroline and Linda froze mid-sip, their noses practically twitching with curiosity.

"Uh," I started, glancing between him and the girls. "Sure."

I followed him down the corridor, my footsteps echoing just slightly beneath the buzz of the overhead lights. It was quieter there.

He didn't say much; he just gestured for me to go in first. His office was small but neat, the kind of space that felt lived in professionally, with books lined on one shelf and a small potted plant doing its best to survive under the light.

Dr. Whitaker closed the door quietly behind us.

He moved around the desk but didn't sit. He stayed standing, arms crossing over his chest like he was bracing himself. The movement shifted his lab coat, revealing the silver threading through the sides of his close-cropped hair.

"What's up?" I asked, my brows furrowing slightly.

"This isn't anything official," he started, his voice calm and careful. "And I want to make that clear. I'm not here in a formal capacity. You haven't done anything wrong."

My shoulders stiffened, even though I tried not to let it show. "Okay..." I replied.

He paused, then sighed quietly. His fingers went to the frames of his glasses, adjusting them as if the words needed better focus. "It's about Noah West."

My heart skipped—just slightly, enough for my brows to lift.

Dr. Whitaker watched me like he was trying to read something beneath my skin. "I know his grandmother is a patient. And I know... things have looked friendly between you two."

He held up a hand before I could interrupt. "Which, again, isn't a violation. There's no policy against seeing a patient's family member. Nothing that technically crosses any line."

He shifted, exhaling slowly. "But from a colleague's point of view, I just wanted to say... be careful. These things can get messy. I've seen it before."

My spine straightened, just a fraction, but it was enough to make the air feel tighter around me.

"Nothing's going on," I said, sharper than I meant to. "We're friends. That's it."

"I'm not saying you've done anything wrong," he said again, gently. "I just wanted to make sure you understood how it can look."

I exhaled through my nose and looked at the floor. This wasn't about policy. It was about perception. And maybe that was worse.

When I glanced back up, he was already stepping aside, as if we were done here—like he'd cleared his conscience.

"I appreciate the... heads-up," I said stiffly.

He nodded once. "That's all I wanted to say."

Caroline and Linda were exactly where I had left them: leaning over the nurse's station like it was the front row of a gossip concert. Their faces shifted the instant they saw me, with concern edging out the teasing.

"What was that about?" Caroline asked, her tone softer now.

I shrugged, trying for casual. "Just... a talk."

Linda straightened. "A talk? With that face? Imara, what did he say?"

I hesitated, then shook my head. "He said to be careful. That things with a patient's family member can get... complicated."

Their expressions dropped into full disapproval mode. Caroline's mouth fell open.

"Oh, hell no."

Linda crossed her arms. "He's just jealous."

I blinked. "What?"

"Please," Caroline scoffed. "The man has been giving you googly eyes ever since you turned him down. Then he saw someone else stepping up, and suddenly it became 'complicated'?"

"If Charlotte had heard this," Linda said, her voice rising with righteous fury, "she would have eaten him alive."

"She'd have had him for breakfast," Caroline agreed. "With a side of 'mind your business.'"

I ran a hand down my face. "Can we not make this into a dramatic soap opera, please? I already feel mortified."

Linda leaned in, her voice softer now. "Hey. You didn't do anything wrong."

"Seriously," Caroline added. "If talking to a hot man who makes you soup is a crime, then lock me up immediately."

Despite everything, I let out a small laugh. Because really—what else could I do?

I glanced down the hallway toward the office I had just left. Then I turned back to the station, let out a sigh, and reached for the next chart.

The moment I lifted it, my phone buzzed in my pocket.

I didn't even try to be subtle. Like some giddy girl who hadn't learned a damn thing, I checked it fast—too fast—because for a split second, my heart did this ridiculous flutter like it was him. Like it was Noah.

But it wasn't. It was... Derek?

I won't give up.

The breath whooshed out of me before I realized I'd been holding it. My fingers tightened around the phone, and my pulse flared with something I couldn't quite name—anger, dread, and disappointment. All of it. Too much of it.

I pressed the side button hard, locking the screen.

What the hell was wrong with this man? I mean, seriously. I hadn't answered a single text. Not a word. Not a breath. And still, he found new ways to wedge himself into my peace like a splinter I thought I'd already pulled out.

I won't give up.

Give up what, Derek? The ghost of a relationship you torched all on your own? The version of me you depended on, drained and left empty? That version didn't exist anymore. I had barely made it out of Virginia, and I sure as hell hadn't followed him to Vermont.

I pressed my phone harder into the counter than necessary, jaw clenched, chest tight with an emotion I didn't even have a name for.

Because here's the thing: I had moved on.

Yes, I had moved on.

Not in some poetic, riding-off-into-the-sunset kind of way, but in the real, steady, moment-by-moment way.

With my friends—my real friends. With Charlotte's chaos, Caroline's unsolicited opinions, and Linda's quietly fierce loyalty. With nights filled with laughter, group calls, snowstorms, and pasta. And Noah.

Noah, who was my friend.

We cooked sometimes.

We talked sometimes.

He gave me too much pie and acted annoyed about it.

I kept showing up and pretended not to count down to the next time I would see him.

But that was friendship?

Right?

...Right, so stay the hell out of my life.

CHAPTER 10: FALLING DEEPER

By the time Noah's knock sounded at my door, the place smelled like garlic, I'd lit the candles, and my nerves were three steps past reasonable.

It wasn't a date—I'd reminded myself of that at least twelve times that night. He cooked last time; I offered to return the favor. Simple. Fair. Just two friends taking turns. But apparently, that hadn't stopped me from scrubbing the stovetop as if it owed me money or fluffing the couch pillows with unnecessary precision.

I'd changed twice—three times, really—and ended up in soft jeans and a sweater I usually reserved for Sundays, the kind that just fitted enough to suggest I tried. Not too much, not too obvious. Still... nice.

My pixie cut behaved on the second attempt. I added a touch of gloss, then stared in the mirror too long, wondering if it was too much—too shiny, too hopeful.

The knock came again.

I smoothed a hand down my side and opened the door.

Noah stood there, his flat-cut hair slightly damp beneath a charcoal beanie. He was wearing a slate blue sweater that fit too well and a small smile on his face.

"Thought you might need dessert," he said, lifting a small paper bag. "Brought your pudding."

There was warmth in his voice—easy and familiar.

I arched a brow. "Is this your way of bribing your way out of doing dishes?"

"Just trying to be a good guest," he replied.

I stepped aside, and he shrugged out of his coat—moving through the door as if he'd done it a dozen times. And maybe that was what threw me— the way he fit there, the way he paused to glance around as if it weren't his first time and wouldn't be his last.

There was a man in my space. A man who didn't flinch at the mess of real life. A man who brought pudding without being asked and listened as if it mattered. A man who looked at me—not past me, not around me, but at me—with a steadiness I was still trying to learn how to hold.

And my brain immediately screamed: FRIENDS.

Friends, Imara.

I shut the door behind us, took a breath, and followed him in, pretending not to notice how my pulse had quickened or how he looked even better with his sleeves pushed to the elbows, already surveying the counter.

"I set the table," I said, motioning to the little setup I had put together in a fit of pre-company anxiety. Napkins folded. Candles lit, and no chaos in sight.

He raised an eyebrow. "Wow. You really went for it."

"I'm capable of class," I said with mock offense as I headed back toward the kitchen. "You just keep seeing me on hospital-adjacent time. There's a difference."

He laughed, and the sound filled the space in a way that made my chest ache a little—because I had missed this.

Not him.

Not love.

Just... this.

We sat at the table I had low-key obsessed over for the last two hours; with the candles, I definitely hadn't pulled out just because I knew he was coming over. They just... matched the vibe. That was all.

Noah took a bite, closed his eyes for half a second, and let out a low, approving hum.

I pointed my fork at him. "Okay, that sound? Illegal."

He opened one eye, amused. "What? It's good."

"Noah," I said.

He smirked and set the fork down, slightly leaning back in his chair. "Alright. It's really good. Better than expected. Dare I say... impressive."

"You say that like you thought I'd serve you dry toast."

"I just figured I'd need to fake it," he teased, his eyes dancing. "Instead, I was debating asking for seconds."

I pretended to mull that over. "Well, I considered poisoning it. So... you might want to pace yourself."

His laugh was low and rough at the edges; it sent a warm little ripple through the air between us. I sipped my wine to hide the smile that threatened my face. His knee brushed mine under the table, and for the first time, I didn't shift away. Neither did he.

"Have you ever been ice fishing?" he asked after a beat, as if he was sitting on the question too long and finally gave in.

"Ice. Fishing. I'm sorry, do I look like someone who'd choose hypothermia for fun?"

He laughed again, leaning forward slightly. "It isn't as dramatic as it sounds. We'd have hot drinks and snacks. I have the gear and a friend's cabin we could use."

I squinted at him. "So... your pitch was: come sit on a frozen lake with me and pray I don't fall in."

He grinned. "I'd even bring the blankets."

"You keep saying we, I have not agreed to this madness."

"You will," he said confidently, eyes gleaming. "You like warm drinks. You are always cold. It checks out."

"First sledding. Now, ice fishing. What is it with you guys forcing me to bond with nature?"

"Character development," he said, and I swore he enjoyed it a little too much. "You can't live here and avoid the full winter package."

"Do I have to touch worms?"

He winced. "I'll handle the bait."

I stared at him for a second longer. He just sat there, relaxed, smug, and honestly, kind of adorable in that "you will cave, and we both know it" way.

And—ugh.

Fine.

Fine.

"Okay," I said, sighing as if it were physically painful. "I'll go. But only because I want to see how ridiculous you looked in snow pants."

He grinned, victorious. "It is a great look. Prepare yourself."

"Remind me again why I said yes to this," I muttered, tightening my scarf until I was one wind gust away from asphyxiation.

"You were charmed by my enthusiasm," Noah called over his shoulder as he trudged through knee-deep snow. "And snacks. You specifically demanded snacks."

Right. Snacks. My weakness.

We trudged across what was apparently a frozen lake—a concept I still hadn't fully accepted—while Noah carried a little sled with gear, a thermos of something hot, and an infuriating amount of cheer for someone who had dragged me into the literal tundra.

He looked good, of course—stupidly good. He'd pulled his beanie low, the cold kissed his cheeks, and his lips curved into a smile that made it seem like he was fighting the urge to laugh every time he glanced back and saw me still alive.

I looked like I was fighting for my life in a padded marshmallow costume. My boots made sad, squeaky noises. My gloves were too big, and my hat itched.

"Are you doing okay back there?" he called out.

"I'm fantastic," I deadpanned. "This is exactly how I wanted to die. Cold. Bitter. Slightly bloated from thermos cocoa."

His warm and unbothered laugh cut through the wind.

By the time we reached the spot, I'd lost feeling in most of my toes and at least one ear. He started setting up near a line of tiny huts like he did every weekend—augering through the ice, unpacking his gear, spreading out blankets. Blankets. The man had even brought blankets.

God, I loved that man.

I mean—not in a "love you" way, but... as a concept. In a normal way. As an expression

"Here," he said, tossing me a hand warmer and gesturing to a folding chair as if it were a relaxing day at the beach.

I settled in slowly and cautiously because I wasn't about to fall through the ice and give everyone a chance to memorialize me as that girl from down south who died chasing a man's approval.

"Okay," I said, glancing down at the hole. "So... what now?"

"Now we wait," he said. "And freeze. And bond with the quiet."

"Mm," I hummed. "I feel so bonded already."

He grinned. "You'll love it."

I rolled my eyes but took the thermos he had offered and leaned back into the blanket-covered chair, letting the stillness settle in.

The lake was quiet in that eerie winter way—just wind and the occasional creak of ice shifting.

And, okay... it wasn't awful.

Noah, for the record, was very determined to prove he was good at this—which was both cute and hilarious because... spoiler alert: he wasn't!

Thirty minutes in, the line hadn't so much as twitched, but Noah adjusted it as if the fish were watching, talked to it, and frowned with intent.

"Are you all right over there, Ice Whisperer?" I asked, sipping cocoa.

"Don't test me," he said without looking up. "Any minute now, I am going to catch a monster, and you will have to eat those words."

"I should have eaten your emergency trail mix and left you there with your pride," I retorted.

He turned to me slowly, one brow raised, and then—he got up. He lumbered toward me in his snow gear with the exaggerated menace of someone about to do something stupid.

"Noah," I laughed, backing away as my boots slipped. "Don't—"

"You mocked me."

"You looked like you were trying to summon a fish telepathically. How was I supposed to take you seriously?"

He lunged, and I squealed, skidding away on boots that were definitely not designed for dodging ice. We both laughed like idiots, slipping and sliding across the surface in a ridiculous dance of revenge and chaos.

Then—crack.

My heart stopped.

There was a sharp, hollow sound under his boots, followed by the sudden, terrifying collapse of ice as it gave out beneath him. "Noah—!" I screamed.

I watched it happen in slow motion as if my brain couldn't catch up. He plunged straight through the surface, and the laughter was cut out of my throat as if someone had snatched it away mid-breath.

"Noah!" I screamed again, dropping to my knees and scrambling toward the edge where the ice had shattered.

He broke the surface a second later, gasping, his eyes wide, the shock written across every inch of his face as his hands clawed at the edge.

"Don't move!" I shouted, already crawling forward on my stomach like I had seen in one of those terrifying outdoor survival videos.

His lips began turning pale, and his arms shook violently.

I inched forward, terrified, and reached for him.

"Take my hand!"

He grabbed it, and I braced myself with everything I had, leaning back slowly, digging my heels into the snow behind me, my heart pounding against my ribs.

Bit by bit, I pulled him out—half-sliding, half-dragging—until he was back on solid ice, dripping, gasping, alive.

We both sat there for a second. Just breathing and being.

"What the hell were you thinking?" I whispered, my breath still ragged, my heart refusing to calm down.

He laughed. He actually laughed, even as his shoulders shook with cold, water dripped from his jacket in miserable little streams, and his eyes fluttered closed as if he were processing what had just happened.

Between gasps of breath and chattering teeth, he grinned. "I've never actually been ice fishing."

I blinked. "I'm sorry, what?"

He cracked one eye open, sheepish and soaked. "I made the whole thing up. I watched two YouTube videos. I just... I thought it'd be a fun way to impress you. I don't know."

My jaw dropped. "Are you kidding me?"

He shrugged—or tried to, which only made his wet coat slosh, and I wanted to scream. "You barely survived sledding, and that left a bad taste in your mouth. I figured I had to step it up before you used that as an excuse never to go out again."

"You figured falling through a lake would make a better impression?"

He winced, his lips pale but twitching into a ghost of a smile. "I wasn't planning on falling."

"Oh, well, that was reassuring," I muttered, grabbing the nearest towel and pressing it to his hair with maybe a little more force than necessary. "Next time, don't flirt with hypothermia. Just hand me a cookie and say you like my smile."

He chuckled under his breath, weak but sincere. "I do like your smile."

I was still kneeling in front of him, toweling off the edges of a man who could have actually died trying to make me laugh—a man who said things like that when he was barely coherent.

I didn't know what to do with it.

So I kept drying his hair, kept my eyes on the towel, and kept my heart from leaping up and making a fool of us both.

Because... that didn't feel like a crush. It didn't feel like a fling or a lonely kind of wanting. It felt safe. Terrifyingly safe.

A beat passed—one I didn't know how to fill.

"I am going to kill you," I said to the clouds.

"Fair," he whispered, still shivering. "Just warm me up first?"

I don't remember how we got back to the car—only that I was practically dragging him, one arm looped under his, his breath loud in my ear, every few steps muttering, "I'm fine," as if I didn't literally feel his body trembling through five layers of clothing.

"You're not fine," I snapped, shoving him into the passenger seat and cranking the heat up so high it was probably illegal. "You were borderline hypothermic and also stupid."

He grinned at me through chattering teeth. "Still worth it."

I didn't respond—mostly out of fear of what would come out of my mouth if I opened it.

The drive was quiet—except for the heater groaning as if it was battling a blizzard and Noah occasionally sniffling as if he was using sheer willpower to hold himself together.

He sank further into the seat, his eyes half-lidded, his jaw clenched.

"You aren't allowed to die trying to impress me," I whispered.

That got a small smile out of him. "So you were impressed."

"Shut up," I murmured, but my voice cracked at the end.

Because I was.

And I hated that I didn't even know where the line was anymore.

"Are you good?" I asked softly.

He nodded, his voice still hoarse. "Warm."

I nodded back.

"I owe you for dragging my frozen corpse out of the lake."

I shrugged. "It is what friends are for."

He watched me for a beat, something unreadable in his expression.

"Okay then," he said as he sat up a little, "to make it up to you and to save the last of my dignity, I'll plan something else."

I narrowed my eyes. "If it involves snow or ice, I'll stage an intervention."

"No snow," he promised. "I was thinking something warmer. Somewhere quieter. A real dinner. A tucked-away spot."

I tilted my head. "Like a restaurant?"

What I really wanted to ask was if it was like a date, but I didn't— because what if it wasn't?

What if I said the word and ruined whatever that fragile, glowing thing was between us?

"Like a restaurant," he confirmed. "That serves actual food—no food cooked over an open fire or eaten with gloves on."

"And you are... inviting me?"

"I am repaying you," he said, his lips twitching. "Don't let it go to your head."

My heart tripped over itself just a little.

But I smirked. "You better not try to impress me this time."

"No promises," he said, sinking back into his chair with a sleepy grin.

CHAPTER 11: FRIENDZONED

Caroline asked, "Soo, what are you wearing tonight?"

I sighed and snapped a mirror selfie; my head tilted just enough to hide the "I've changed twice" bags under my eyes; the lighting adjusted so that the one good lamp in my apartment did its job.

Black turtleneck. Dark jeans. Chunky boots.

Charlotte then said, "Why do you look like you are going to read poetry at your niece's christening??"

Linda exclaimed, "Girl, what is this?"

Caroline repeated, "Imara."

Then Caroline almost yelled, "IMARA."

I looked in the mirror again, defensively. I looked fine. Clean, sophisticated, and slightly artistic, like someone who owned a journal and maybe a favorite mug. And also—importantly—not someone who was trying too hard for what was, allegedly, just a casual dinner.

Two minutes later, the group call came in. I stared at the screen as if it had personally betrayed me.

Charlotte's face filled the screen first. "You look like a high-functioning librarian with a fear of color," she said.

Caroline leaned in from her square, pointing her spoon like it was a mic. "Be honest—are you going to dinner or filing tax documents under candlelight?"

Linda groaned, flopping dramatically onto her pillow. "That is giving funeral vibes, not flirty."

"I wasn't trying to flirt!" I snapped, clutching at the fabric as if it would defend me. "It is just dinner. He almost froze to death. It is a thank-you-for-not-letting-me-die dinner."

Caroline narrowed her eyes. "Imara. You cooked for this man. You have seen his torso in full high-definition. And now you are dressing like a chaperone for a seventh-grade dance?"

"I look respectable," I said.

"You look like you are gently going to recommend someone read The Bell Jar and then knit them a blanket," Charlotte said flatly.

"I like my sweater!" I defended.

Caroline snorted. "No, babe. You survived in that sweater. You did taxes in that sweater. You do not go on emotionally confusing Vermont dinners in that sweater."

"I don't even know if it's a date!"

All three of them said, "It's a date," at the same time as if they had rehearsed it.

I sighed and held up another outfit option—this time a midi dress with a cardigan, praying it would buy me peace.

Charlotte immediately winced. "Are you trying to repel him?"

"Oh my God," I muttered, dragging a hand over my face.

Linda zoomed in. "Is that a mauve cardigan?"

Caroline literally gagged. "Okay. Everyone breathe. We were going to get through this."

And somehow, without even knowing how, I let them style me from across the town.

By the end of the call, I was in high-waisted black pants, a fitted cream top, boots with a little heel, and a cropped jacket I had forgotten I owned.

"Better," Charlotte declared. "Now, do your makeup like you are about to be kissed in a parking lot."

"YOU'RE ALL INSANE," I exclaimed.

Caroline just grinned. "You're welcome."

They hung up the call in a flurry of chaos, screaming, and aggressive encouragement. Silence fell over my apartment like a thick wool blanket.

I stared at my reflection in the mirror for a beat too long.

Okay. I looked... good.

Not desperate, thirst-trap-good, but like an adult woman who owned skincare and had opinions about pasta-shaped goods.

Still, my stomach felt coiled and tight.

I shouldn't have been nervous. I shouldn't have felt nervous.

It was dinner.

With Noah.

Who was my friend?

My completely platonic, emotionally stable, stubbornly endearing friend who made homemade sauces, fell through frozen lakes, brought me pie, and smiled at me as if I were more than background noise.

Cool. Great. Awesome.

I swallowed hard, then started pacing my living room as if it would shake the feelings loose. I checked the clock—again—and then once more, just to be sure it hadn't magically fast-forwarded through the most awkward five minutes of my life.

What if I got in the car and said something weird?

What if I tripped in the parking lot?

What if that was just normal to him, and I was the only one who had been internally monologuing for three weeks straight?

The knock at the door startled me so hard that I nearly flung my phone into the kitchen sink.

I smoothed a hand over my hair, muttered something that was probably not a prayer but close, and pulled the door open.

And I immediately forgot how to breathe.

He was wearing a button-up shirt that fit entirely too well; his sleeves were rolled just enough to show forearms I had absolutely no business noticing, his collar open. His skin practically glowed under the porch light—deep brown, smooth, and infuriatingly perfect.

All I could think about was the fact that I had seen what was under that shirt. I had not just imagined it. I had seen it. I had felt it when I was dragging him out of that lake. His flushed and cold skin was far too easy to think about now.

My stomach did a full somersault.

He wasn't even trying. He was just standing there like some cursed blend of a Calvin Klein ad and a Sunday brunch dream boy.

"Hey," he said, his voice a low, warm thing that slid straight into my bones.

"Hi," I replied.

His eyes roamed, slow and intentional. They took their time, but when they landed back on mine, they were softer.

"You look..." He trailed off, tilting his head just slightly. "Really good."

I would not melt. I would not melt.

I raised an eyebrow because deflection was a survival tactic. "Wow. Actual praise? Do I need to write that down?"

"You can't just take a compliment, can you?" he replied.

He leaned in slightly—not close enough to touch, but close enough that I felt the heat radiating off his skin, close enough to smell whatever cologne he was wearing. Or maybe it was just him—that same mix of citrus and coffee and the kind of warmth that made you want to lean into it without thinking.

His eyes moved slowly across my face, pausing at my mouth, jaw, and eyes. My chest rose and fell too fast. Too telling. He wet his bottom lip—slowly. Thoughtfully. Then he breathed in, deep and quiet.

I felt everything.

A soft ache in my stomach. The prickling heat behind my knees. That tight, low tug that shouldn't have been happening. Not from just... breathing.

I held my breath like that would stop my body's reaction, as if I wasn't seconds away from forgetting every boundary I had ever put in place.

"Let's go," he murmured. "I really want to show you this spot."

Just like that.

Like the air between us hadn't just shifted. Like I wasn't still holding on to oxygen and hadn't remembered how to release it.

Because words felt too dangerous, I nodded and followed him out the door.

Still reeling. Still burning.

And very much aware that I might have already been in trouble.

The restaurant was exactly what he had said it would be: cozy, quiet, and tucked away from the busy streets.

Warm light spilled from little lamps and twinkling light strings wrapped around wooden beams. The walls were old wood and colorful panels that gave the place a laid-back, artsy vibe.

A server led us to a corner booth, half-hidden by a tree growing through the floor, with lights hanging down like stars. Noah waited for me to slide in first, then sat across from me, leaning back as if genuinely settled.

I fidgeted with my napkin until the waiter brought water and menus, and I had the opportunity not to be perceived for thirty seconds.

"Do you come here a lot?" I asked.

Noah shook his head, glancing around. "Not really. Once or twice. Came alone both times."

I tilted my head. "Alone?"

He shrugged like it wasn't a big deal. "Sometimes I like the quiet. The drinks are good. They have jazz players on Fridays—real mellow stuff. It's nice just... sitting in it, you know?"

"I get it." I nodded.

Noah ordered with annoying ease—of course, he knew what was good. Of course, he had already scoped out the dessert. I picked something with cheese and garlic, hoping it would ground me before my nervous system short-circuited again.

Halfway through the meal—somewhere between a bite of something amazing and him telling me about the time Mrs. Carter had tried to join a knitting circle purely to spy on a neighbor—he paused.

"I'm always talking about my grandmother," he said, setting down his fork. "But I don't know anything about your family."

"Oh," I said, blinking. "Well, what do you want to know about them?"

"Anything. Everything. Jus—whatever you think I should know."

He waited.

"Well," I said finally, "my mom is the loud one: the first to cry during church and the last to leave any gathering. She always smells like cocoa butter and peppermint.

My dad's the opposite: quiet and thoughtful. He listens more than he speaks. He used to write me little notes and tuck them into my lunch, even when I was in college." I paused, my eyes fixed on my glass. "I still have a few."

A smile tugged at my mouth before I could help it. "My parents are high school sweethearts, if you can believe it. They still do matching outfits every Easter like it's their job. Same color schemes, coordinated shoes, the whole thing. It's embarrassing in the cutest way."

"It sounds ironic. I wish you had pictures."

I reached into my bag and pulled out my phone, swiping through the photos until I found one from last Easter—my mom in a sunshine yellow dress with giant puff sleeves and my dad in a matching polo with a grin so big it could've powered a city.

I slid the phone across the table.

Noah took it and leaned in, his mouth twitching with amusement. "You look nothing like your mom," he said. "You're all your dad— eyes, smile, even the brows."

"It was a moment," I laughed, curling my fingers around my glass.

He smiled, softer now. "Sounds like they really love each other."

"They do," I said, and my chest tightened as I did. "My dad's still obsessed with my mom. Can you imagine he hand-writes lyrics from old soul songs and leaves them on her pillow? Isn't that kind of obsessed? The man stays in his feelings."

"Romance isn't dead," he murmured.

"Nope. Not if you ask my dad." I swirled what was left of my drink in the glass, watching the light catch the rim. "They're back home. Two states away. I haven't seen them in a while."

That caught his attention.

His gaze sharpened—not nosy, not pushy. Just... aware. Like he was tucking that piece of information into a quiet file marked Important.

"Virginia, right. What made you move all the way here?" he asked.

I shook my head. "Nope, not moved. This is just a stop on the tour."

He lifted an eyebrow.

"I'm a travel nurse," I explained, leaning back. "They placed me here for six months. Technically, I've got about three left before they ask where I want to go next."

He went still for a second, and it felt like just enough information had dropped into the space between us to tilt the balance.

"You're leaving?" he asked, his voice low.

"Eventually," I drawled, tucking a stray strand behind my ear. "That's the job. Go where you're needed. Pack up. Start fresh. Although there's an option for me to stay here permanently, I just... I'm not sure yet."

"You don't like it here?" he asked carefully.

"No," I said quickly, then shook my head. "I mean, I do like it much more than I expected, honestly. Vermont's been... well, surprising."

He tilted his head. "Surprising how?"

I shrugged, forcing a small smile. "I came here to work and fill a role. I didn't expect to make friends, start baking again, orfind my rhythm so fast. It's just... weird, I guess."

"Not weird," he said. "You're allowed to like where you land."

I met his gaze across the table.

He said it so simply. So evenly. Like it wasn't a big deal.

But something about it hit me square in the chest.

Maybe it was the way he had said it that made it feel like he was trying to believe the same thing.

Maybe it was the way he hadn't pushed or tried to sell me on staying.

Maybe it was the way he had just let me think about it without expectation.

"I haven't stayed anywhere this long... ever," I said quietly.

"You could," he replied, just as soft. "If you wanted to. I hadn't realized you were passing through," he said softly.

I lifted my eyes to meet his.

Before it had gotten too heavy, the waiter appeared with dessert, which was some warm, ridiculous chocolate thing Noah had insisted on ordering because "You don't say no to molten cake, Imara."

And okay, fine, he was right. Again.

He dived into it like it was a competition. I took a bite and moaned out loud.

"You're disgusting," he said, grinning.

"You're just mad I got the better side."

"We're sharing one plate."

"Exactly."

We bickered until the cake was half gone, and the moment lightened and loosened around us like an exhale.

He leaned back, his eyes flicking toward the low-lit windows. "I've been thinking about expanding the café," he said, almost absently. "Adding more seating and maybe doing weekend brunches. It's been doing better than I thought, and I guess I... want to give it a real shot. If you... stuck around; maybe you could help me figure it out. I mean, give your opinion. Be a sounding board."

My face heated immediately. "Noah—" I let out a quiet laugh, half nervous, half flustered. "I don't know anything about baking. Or design. Or business expansion."

He shrugged, still watching me. "You don't need to. A little moral support from you might be all I need."

I ducked my head, fighting the smile that had already been curling at my mouth. "You're just trying to get free labor."

"I'm trying to keep the good things close," he said, soft but sure.

The good things... was that me?

Did he... like me like that? Because it had been easy—great, even—but maybe I was reading too much into the glances, the meals, and the way his eyes found me even in a crowded room.

Maybe that was just how he was: warm and attentive. Maybe he was the kind of man who knew how to make you feel like the only person in the room.

And maybe I was so far out of the game that I started seeing sparks where there had only been comfort.

There was a beat of quiet. It was not awkward; just enough space to second-guess every choice I'd made since putting on lip gloss.

He sipped his drink like he hadn't just tilted my whole world slightly on its axis.

I leaned my chin on my hand, watching him go on about a new espresso machine he was thinking about buying, maybe hiring someone part-time to help with the morning rush so he could be around Mrs. Carter more.

There was a beat of comfortable quiet. And before I even thought about it, I tilted my head.

"You know," I said casually, "you either talk about work or your grandmother. What about you?"

His brow lifted slightly. "What do you mean?"

"Like... your life," I said, twirling my spoon lazily. "Do you ever think about getting married? Having kids? Or is your plant to live off espresso and sass forever?"

His smile flickered.

Just a little.

His fingers paused around the rim of his mug, and his gaze dropped.

"I don't know," he said finally, his voice quieter than before.

I blinked. "You've never thought about it?"

"Oh, I've thought about it," he said with a dry laugh that hadn't quite reached his eyes. "I just... don't really see it working out for me."

"Why not?" I asked gently.

"I've got the café and Mrs. Carter. That's enough," he said like it was a full stop. Like he was quietly closing the door on something before it creaked open too far.

But just when I thought he might say more or crack the window even an inch, he exhaled and shifted casually but purposefully.

"But what about you?" he asked, tilting his head, his voice smooth again. "Do you see yourself with the whole white-picket-fence situation?"

I opened my mouth, ready to say the usual thing. The safe thing.

I have been focusing on myself; my career was the priority, and I didn't have time for anything else.

I wanted to say that the last time I let someone in like that nearly broke me. So I wasn't in a rush to do it again.

But the words hadn't come.

Instead, I hesitated.

And I never hesitated.

Not on that. Not when I'd said it a hundred times. Not when I was repeating that story to myself for months like it was gospel truth.

Noah watched me carefully. Not pushing. Just... waiting.

And maybe that was what made it worse.

Because I didn't know why the answer suddenly felt off, I cleared my throat, forcing a smile.

"I mean... I'm just trying to keep my houseplants alive right now."

He laughed softly, not calling me out on the dodge. "Bold of you to assume that anyone would trust you with succulents."

"They're dramatic!" I protested. "They act fine for three weeks and then just die out of nowhere."

Noah chortled and shook his head, sliding his card to the waiter. He didn't push or ask again, which somehow made me wish he would have.

The night air bit us when we stepped outside. He opened the passenger door for me, and I climbed in, settling into the warmth like I hadn't been battling high tension since dessert.

He joined me a moment later, the car humming softly to life. A faint playlist murmured from the speakers—something acoustic.

The road wound gently ahead, snowbanks glowing under the streetlights. I stole glances at him—one hand on the wheel, the other resting casually on the gearshift.

He hadn't said much since I dodged his question.

And the thing was... I didn't know why I hesitated. It had never happened before. I had given that same speech a hundred times, practiced, and polished it like I had laminated and memorized it. I said it and moved on.

Tonight, it felt like a lie I didn't believe anymore.

"You got quiet," Noah said eventually, his eyes still on the road.

I shrugged, my fingers twisting in my lap. "Just thinking."

He didn't ask what. He just nodded, thoughtful.

"You don't have to have it all figured out," he said, his voice low. "Even if everyone expects you to."

I wanted to say something. Anything.

Instead, I just nodded once, slowly.

And the rest of the drive hummed with quiet understanding: No big declarations or more questions.

We pulled up outside my place, and for a second, neither of us moved.

He reached across me, slow and sure, his fingers brushing the clasp of my seatbelt. His knuckles grazed my coat and ribs, and the fabric between us was suddenly insufficient.

Click.

The belt snapped free, but his hand hadn't immediately pulled back.

And neither had I.

I looked at him. He was close enough for me to count the gold flecks in his eyes and feel the heat coming off him in waves.

"I could've unbuckled myself, you know."

His gaze flicked to my mouth the second the words left it. And then back up. His voice dropped, rough and a little too smooth.

"Where's the fun in that?"

His fingers were still so close to my ribs that I felt the pressure of his presence more than his touch. My breath hitched, my chest rising in a shallow inhale I hadn't quite been able to hide. Everything in the car felt still and tight, like a live wire of tension humming between us.

He pulled away suddenly, taking the warmth with him, got out, and rounded the car to open my door as if it had been just chivalry, not something heavier. I closed my eyes and snapped my teeth together.

I swung my legs out slowly, my boots crunching into the snow, and he walked me to the door.

I stopped at the top of the steps and turned toward him, my eyes searching. I could hear my heart thudding in my ears faster than it should have been.

I shouldn't have. I knew I shouldn't have. But the night had gone so well, and now my body was doing all these wildly inappropriate things—like leaning toward him without my permission and imagining how his mouth would have felt pressed against mine. My brain was trying to be reasonable, but my heart had gone rogue, and my hormones were throwing a damn parade.

My body would give in if he leaned in again, even the slightest tilt. I didn't care if it was a mistake. I needed to know what it felt like. I needed—

He looked at me, soft and quiet in the dim porch light. His eyes warm. His lips slightly parted.

This was it.

"Goodnight, friend."

I stared at him.

No, stared was too soft. I mentally drop-kicked him into the sun while physically standing there like someone had unplugged my soul.

Friend?

Friend?

I nodded and smiled like a well-adjusted adult.

"Goodnight."

CHAPTER 12: THAWING

A whole day off.

That day, I would have given anything to be elbow-deep in patient charts or elbowed in the ribs by Mr. Harlan because "You remind me of my ex-wife who ruined my credit but made a mean meatloaf."

Because, at least at the hospital, my brain had a purpose. I was too busy counting meds, monitoring vitals, and dodging emotional landmines to notice how empty my house felt. Or how everything smelled like the candle I lit before getting dressed up for a date that technically wasn't a date. Or how my lips still tingled from a kiss that did not happen.

I mean, really. Friend?

I had tried to distract myself for the past two hours. Laundry. Cleaning out the fridge. I even tried reorganizing my bookshelf by color, like I was some Pinterest mom with a minimalist aesthetic and a stable emotional state. Spoiler: I wasn't.

I flopped onto the couch with a dramatic sigh so loud it startled the cat that didn't live here but somehow visited me every other day like it paid rent.

I stared at the ceiling.

My phone buzzed against my leg. Again. And again.

I ignored it the first two times. I was mid-spiral and honestly kind of enjoying the drama of pretending no one understood me.

But on the third buzz, I glanced at the screen.

Linda:

"How's our wounded warrior? Are you eating today or just stress-cleaning the grout?"

Charlotte:

"She's 100% still spiraling. Bet she alphabetized her spice rack by mood."

Caroline:

"Not to stir the cauldron, but Beau brought me a smoothie this morning and kissed my third eye before he left. Just saying. Love can be real. Sometimes. If you squint."

I groaned and flopped back on the couch. These women were psychic. Or nosy. Or both.

Me:

"I'm fine. Just ignoring my feelings like the emotionally avoidant goddess I am."

Linda:

"Mmm. Lies with a hint of cinnamon. What's really going on?"

Charlotte:

"You want me to come over and light something on fire? Because I will. Metaphorically."

Caroline

"You know I love you, babe, but take a walk. Touch something alive. Like a tree. Or a man with actual follow-through. Preferably both."

I was about to roll my eyes when a sharp crack rattled against the window like something mean had just slapped it.

I froze and turned slowly.

The outside had turned into a snow globe from hell.

The wind howled like it wanted to be inside. Hail pinged off the porch rail like someone was throwing marbles, and the snow was coming down fast—thick and sideways, blurring the world into white static.

Great. Now, I was getting emotionally and literally snowed in.

Me:

"Change of plans. I'm not taking a walk unless it's across the River Styx. Pretty sure Elsa is having a rage fit outside."

Caroline:

"Yikes. Stay inside. Wrap yourself in something cozy. Drink something warm. Let the feelings pass through you like a moon cycle."

Charlotte:

"Or drink whiskey and rewatch a show where no one gets friend-zoned."

Linda:

"Weather like that makes people think things they shouldn't. Don't let the storm trick you into texting him."

Me:

"It's not that bad. I'm totally fine. Not texting. Just… maybe watching the snow and reevaluating every life choice I've ever made."

Caroline:

"That's the spirit! It's emotional catharsis, but make it cute."

Charlotte:

"We love a woman who feels deeply and suffers privately. You'll survive. But just in case—charge your phone and don't do anything heroic."

Linda:

"And if you get snowed in for real, remember—this isn't the Oregon Trail. You have snacks and Wi-Fi."

Despite myself, I smiled even as the wind shrieked against the window again like it was trying to pick a fight.

I walked over to the front door and peeked through the curtain like something evil was haunting me. The world outside was white. Blinding white. Apocalyptic blizzard white.

Was he at the hospital with Mrs. Carter?

Was he holed up in his café, checking pipes and sipping something dark and unnecessarily poetic like black coffee with a hint of guilt?

Did he really walk me to my door, look at me like that, and think it was nothing and we were just... friends?

I knew I was misreading the signs. I knew better. And yet, there I was, practically swooning on my porch like I was starring in my private romance.

He was just walking his friend to the door.

I sighed, dragged the blanket up to my chin, and flipped a page I knew I'd have to reread later. Defeated, I closed the book entirely and let it rest on my chest.

Outside, the wind howled like a woman scorned.

My phone buzzed.

I glanced at it, assuming it was Charlotte again, with some *men who are canceled* memes or Caroline sending a picture of Beau being tragically shirtless in the snow.

But it wasn't them.

Noah:

"You snowed in?"

Suddenly, I was wide awake. Blanket forgotten. The book slid to the floor like it knew it was about to be abandoned.

Should I answer? Would it be weird not to?

I mean, it was a simple, polite, and friendly question, which was apparently the only language Noah spoke now.

I tossed the phone onto the couch like it had personally offended me, then immediately lunged for it again because what if he was waiting for a reply?

Me:

"Yeah... it's getting pretty bad out there. The wind sounds like it's ready to peel the siding off the house.

Ten minutes passed.

Maybe less.

Maybe a thousand years.

No reply.

He was probably busy. Maybe Mrs. Carter was the one who even asked him to reach out. I started to reach for my book again, pretending to be calm, when I heard—

Scrape.

I froze.

Scrape... scrape...

I stood slowly, heart thudding.

Shoveling.

Outside my door.

I tiptoed to the window and pulled back the curtain just enough to peek through. And there he was.

Noah was there. Hood up. Shoulders hunched against the wind. Shovel in hand. Clearing a path through the snow like it was the most normal thing in the world.

He cleared the last few feet, breath misting in the air as he straightened up, shovel scraping one final time before he leaned on it—just for a second.

Buzz.

I glanced down.

Noah:

"You gonna let me in or just keep staring like I'm a weather mirage?"

My hand flew to the door handle so fast you'd think I was waiting my whole life for this moment.

The door swung open.

Cold rushed in. So did he.

I stood there, blinking at him like I had forgotten how to function. My voice caught somewhere between my chest and throat, and what came out was half laugh, half breath, full disbelief.

"You're out of your mind."

He shrugged, stamping snow off his boots. "Probably."

I shook my head, that stunned little laugh slipping out again, softer this time. My fingers tightened around the doorframe like I needed it to steady me.

This was the part no one warned you about.

When the guy you'd been trying not to like showed up—literally—in a snowstorm, like some slow-burn fever dream. When he brought you food and kept finding excuses to sit near you when he said we were friends but acted like we were more.

And the worst part?

You started to want him to be more.

I wasn't stupid. I knew how this went.

I knew what it felt like to fall for someone who was already halfway out the door.

But I also knew what it meant when a man kept showing up. And if I was right—even half right—then I had to be careful.

Because I thought I liked Noah.

And if he didn't feel the same way?

Then, I would do what I always did.

Smile and close the door.

CHAPTER 13: WARMING UP

I handed him the tea, the mug warm between his palms, steam curling between us. His jacket hung by the door, dripping slowly onto the mat. He had a blanket folded over his lap—the same one I curled up with during rainy Sunday reruns and pretended it didn't matter because no one ever shared it with me.

I sat across from him, legs tucked up, one hand cradling a mug as if it might buy me time. It didn't.

"So…" I said, staring at the top of my tea. "Not that the whole snowstorm grand gesture didn't touch me, but… why are you here?"

He shifted on the couch, his long frame angling slightly toward me. One arm draped lazily along the back cushion, the other wrapped around the mug resting against his chest. The blanket covered his lap like he was trying to play it casual, but the way his foot tapped lightly against the hardwood said otherwise.

The TV hummed in the background, volume low, casting flickering shadows of some cooking show neither of us was watching. My living room felt smaller then.

"I was a little worried," he said, shrugging. "I saw how bad it was getting out there. I've lived through enough of these to know when it goes from pretty to dangerous, and this was your first one." His gaze lifted to mine, soft. "Knowing you're here alone didn't sit right with me."

My heart did something traitorous. It stuttered, and I gripped my mug a bit harder, trying to ground myself. It was stupid, really—how just a few words from him, spoken softly in the middle of a storm, could stir up everything I'd tried to quiet since our last dinner.

My eyes flicked to his mouth before I could stop them, remembering the space that almost wasn't there.

Friends, Imara. Friends worried about each other. Friends shoveled snow. Friends marched through a literal blizzard and showed up on your doorstep with cold fingers and hot tea energy.

It was totally normal and totally fine.

I wrapped both hands around my mug like that was going to ground me. "Well. I'm fine. You didn't have to trek through all that."

"I know," he said, quiet but certain. "I wanted to.

And just like that, my heart skipped again.

His leg was still bouncing—restless, nervous, maybe—but the rest of him was still. His gaze flicked to the TV again, then back to me for a second too long. He sipped his tea as if he hadn't just lit a fuse and decided to sit next to it, waiting for me to react.

Normally, conversation flowed easily with him. And maybe it was me; maybe it was the fact that I thought he would kiss me that night, and my brain hadn't stopped rewriting the ending ever since.

I gently set my mug on the table and grabbed the remote, flipping to something else before the silence got too loud.

Onscreen, a woman stood under the awning of a coffee shop, arms folded tightly across her chest, as the rain pattered all around her. Her voice was low, tight with frustration.

"I kept showing up. Even when you didn't call, even when you made it hard. I was still there."

A man shifted his weight, his eyes tired. "And I never asked you to be. That's the part you keep skipping."

I winced. "Yikes."

Noah let out a quiet scoff, shaking his head. "People stay when it's easy. That's just how it is."

I glanced over, confused. "What do you mean?"

He leaned back, eyes still on the screen. "She wanted him to fight, right? But some people don't fight when they're scared. They freeze. Or run. Doesn't mean they didn't care."

I narrowed my eyes. "So, you're defending the guy who bailed?"

Noah shrugged one shoulder. "I'm saying maybe he didn't know how to show up the way she wanted."

I let out a breath, sharp and low. "Right. And meanwhile, she's sitting there, breaking her heart trying to make it work, thinking he'd stop running if she just loved him enough. Does that sound healthy to you?"

He didn't answer. He just sipped his tea and stared at the screen like it suddenly fascinated him.

His jaw tensed for a beat. "Have you ever had someone leave because they didn't know how to stay? Not because they didn't want to, but because it was easier to walk than to risk staying and being told they weren't enough?"

"I haven't," I replied because they would much rather cheat and use me than do me the justice of walking away.

He swallowed, his voice lower now. "Breakups don't just suck. To me, they felt like confirmation that I would always be temporary, no matter how good it was for a while. That people loved pieces of me, not the whole thing."

I studied him, my fingers trailing absently over the curve of my leg, tracing patterns into the fabric of my sweatpants.

"And before you say it," he continued, "I know that's probably dramatic. I know I've got good people now—my grandmother, the café, you... and the other friends at the hospital." He trailed off, his gaze faltering. "But that voice doesn't really go away. The one that tells me not to get too used to things because eventually, people leave."

I didn't speak right away. I didn't have anything wise or profound to say.

Because I got it.

I knew what it was like to carry the weight of someone else's absence as if it were my fault—to believe you were hard to hold onto, even when all you had ever done was try.

After a second, I nodded and, almost without thinking, shifted from my end of the couch to his—just a few inches at first, then a few more.

Noah shifted his arm along the back of the couch to give me room. I hesitated, my hands fidgeting in my lap. I could feel his heat beside me—not quite touching, but close enough that it hummed in the air between us. He turned, giving me his full focus but without rushing or asking. Just waiting.

"I've only been with one person my whole life," I said. "And I think they used that against me—the not knowing, the benefit of the doubt. They dragged me through the worst of it, and when they finally tried to fight for me, it was already too late. I didn't recognize myself in the mirror anymore, and nothing they said made up for what they took."

Noah's jaw tightened as his eyes scanned mine, memorizing that moment. His thumb brushed along his palm once, then stilled. His voice dipped, firmer now.

"But I wish it wasn't true. I wish life didn't have to play out the same way over and over. Because sometimes," his gaze never left mine, "you run into something so good it makes you forget the odds. It makes you wish the ending could be different this time.

The wind outside howled low against the window, and snow fell in soft sheets. The glow from the TV flickered across his face, painting shadows that shifted and settled. The faint hum of dialogue faded into the background—just noise.

"Some people do get different endings," I murmured, my fingers brushing the edge of the blanket still folded on my lap. "Real and healthy ones. The kind where it doesn't fall apart just because you want more."

His throat bobbed as if he were swallowing something down. He shook his head, eyes narrowing slightly. "Why do you make it so damn easy to bare myself?"

I found myself startled by the question, my eyebrows knitting together. "I don't know," I finally said, my voice barely above a whisper.

He leaned forward and rested his elbows on his knee. His gaze locked onto the floor as if he were trying to summon courage from some hidden place in the wood's grain. "I beat myself up about that night," he said. "On the porch. After dinner. I've played it back a dozen times."

He muttered under his breath and glanced away for a split second before finding me again. "I wanted to kiss you so bad it made my head spin."

My heart kicked hard against my ribs, thudding as if it were trying to escape. My fingers tightened around the edge of the blanket. My lips parted on instinct, not for words, just for air.

His hand lifted, slow and uncertain, before it finally reached me. He cupped my cheek, his palm warm and rough from work.

The flicker of the TV faded into nothing. I didn't hear it anymore. I heard nothing but the rush of blood in my ears and the shallow, nervous breath caught behind my ribs.

His mouth was so close that I could feel the warmth of his breath, taste the hesitation.

His eyes flickered over mine, searching. For what, I didn't know. Permission, maybe. A sign. A reason not to pull away.

My pulse skittered. I felt it in my throat, my fingertips, everywhere.

His eyes dropped to my mouth, and my lips parted. I swore, for a second, we were both holding our breath.

He was going to kiss me.

His eyes widened. Barely—a flicker, like something inside him suddenly slammed the brakes.

I went still

His hand fell from my cheek as if he regretted ever touching me. The cold rushed in instantly, and with it came humiliation, sharp and fast.

He pulled back, just slightly at first—then he stood abruptly, as if sitting there with me, with everything hanging between us, had suddenly become unbearable.

He ran a hand through his hair like he was trying to scrub the moment off his skin. "This isn't…" His voice was hoarse, shaky. "It's not the right time. I shouldn't be doing this."

I swallowed hard. My voice wobbled when I spoke. "Right. Of course."

He didn't even look at me, even though I gave him full eye contact, practically begging for a flicker of that guy from five seconds ago, the one who had leaned in and wanted me.

"I didn't mean to—" he started but stopped.

Spoiler alert: it wasn't fine. It was the opposite of fine. It was a flaming pile of why-do-I-always-fall-for-the-almosts.

He grabbed his coat as if we were in some dramatic indie film but paused at the door like he was considering delivering one last devastating line, but I beat him to it. Because, unfortunately for him, I still had my pride.

"See you around," I said, soft and breezy, as if I was totally cool and not dying inside. An iconic performance.

I hopped up, opened the door before he could say whatever would have made it worse, and let the freezing air slap me in the face instead of him.

He stepped into the snow without another word, and I quietly and gently shut the door behind him as if I hadn't just closed it on one of the worst almost-kisses of my life.

Then I leaned against the door, blinked at the ceiling, and tried to breathe.

My chest ached. My face burned. And my brain already screamed:

Why did I let him touch me? Why did I think maybe this time would be different? Why was I like this?

I told myself I was relieved that I had dodged something messy. That it was better that way. Lies. All of it.

I wasn't relieved. I was humiliated. I was soft. And I was officially a card-carrying member of the "Girl Who Got Ghosted by a Guy Who Almost Kissed Her in a Snowstorm" club.

No one ever talked about how much that sucked.

CHAPTER 14: COOKING

My forehead was flat against the break room table. I was groaning in intervals for the past five minutes, long, pathetic whale sounds that made Caroline keep glancing over as if I were about to burst into flames.

"I can't believe I almost kissed him," I mumbled into the cold plastic. "And he fooled me again. My gosh, can I look any more desperate?"

Which, honestly, wouldn't have been the worst thing that had happened that week.

Linda slid her coffee across the table toward me like a peace offering or a sedative.

"Honey, you didn't almost kiss him. He almost kissed you. You were just sitting there, being all gorgeous and emotionally available. That's not your fault. That's a trap he walked into voluntarily."

"I leaned in, Linda," I protested.

"You're human."

"He said he wanted to kiss me so bad it made his head spin."

"Okay, Shakespeare," Caroline muttered, mouth full of granola. "And yet, somehow, he still didn't."

"I know!" I wailed, lifting my head just long enough to clutch the air dramatically. "Do you have any idea how deeply embarrassing it is for a man you want to kiss you to almost kiss you only for him to turn around and reject you in 4k?"

"It was your living room," Linda said gently.

"Same difference. The trauma is in HD."

Caroline leaned against the counter with her arms crossed, full big-sister mode activated. "Listen. You're gorgeous. You're smart. You're saving lives with mediocre hospital coffee in your system and maybe six hours of sleep a week. You do not have time to be getting emotionally wrecked by a man who doesn't even know how to finish a sentence."

Linda hummed, "Or a kiss."

I dropped my head again with a muffled scream.

"I was wrong to get confused. I thought— I thought we were... I don't know. Something."

"You were something," Linda said gently. "You are something. And it's okay that your heart reacted."

"My heart needs to be quieter," I muttered into the wood grain.

Linda scoffed, "No. It doesn't. It's been through hell, and it's still warm. That's not weakness, that's beautiful."

Caroline jumped in, her tone softer now. "You weren't wrong for feeling something. You weren't wrong for hoping, even if he didn't say it out loud. You're human, Imara. And the fact that your heart still does that little stretch thing means it's still alive. Still open."

I sat up finally, pressing the coffee cup to my face as if it could erase my entire memory. "I hate that I even care this much. He was never mine to begin with."

Caroline rolled her eyes. "Yeah, well. That doesn't mean it didn't feel like something. And for what it's worth, I've seen the way he looks at you when he thinks you're not paying attention. That man's got it bad."

"Then why didn't he kiss me?" I whispered.

They both went quiet for a second. Linda sighed, "Because," she said, "some men don't trust good things when they're standing right in front of them. Especially when those good things are emotionally intelligent, stunning, and a little terrifying in scrubs."

Linda nodded and, already rising to grab her coat, added, "Now, seriously. Stop beating yourself up and go home before we have to drag you out of here like a toddler after nap time."

"I'm not brooding," I mumbled, even as I rubbed the back of my neck and sighed into my tea again. It was cold, just like my night.

I rolled my eyes, tugged on my jacket, and braced for the reality of waiting outside. The one where I walked home alone. Again. Because I was too proud to call anyone and too tired to explain. And Elsa was clearly still throwing a tantrum because the wind was nothing short of feral lately.

"God, I hate walking in this weather," I muttered, zipping up my jacket.

"Blame the patriarchy," Caroline called from behind me.

"Blame Vermont," Linda added, shivering into her scarf.

I just waved them off with a tired smile and pushed open the door.

The wind hit like a slap. I squinted against the sudden rush of cold air, tugged my scarf higher, and tucked my gloved hands into my pockets as if I could brace myself against everything: the snow, the ache in my chest, or the sound of my footsteps echoing a little too loudly in the stillness.

Leaning against the side of his truck, like he wasn't the reason I had spent the last twenty-four hours spiraling into my couch cushions, was Noah.

Noah.

He had one boot crossed over the other, arms folded, his breath fogging in the cold. He looked smug. But also not; he looked like he was trying to be cool but wasn't totally sure if he was allowed to be. Maybe this had seemed like a good idea when he was still in the car, and now he was thinking twice.

My stomach flipped. And not the cute kind of flip—the oh-no kind. The what-in-the-fresh-hell-is-this kind.

I stopped in my tracks and squinted, just in case the cold was making me hallucinate hot, emotionally unavailable men with strong forearms and poor timing.

But no, he was still there.

He straightened when he saw me and gave a slow nod, almost hesitant, like I was a deer and he was trying not to spook me.

What was happening? Why was he here? After that night? After the almost kiss, the even worse almost conversation, and the "I'm not ready" speech?

"Noah," I said, cautious.

"Hold on," he said, pushing off the truck. "Before you say anything, I know you have every right to be mad—"

"I'm not mad." My voice came out sharper than I intended, so I softened it. "I'm not mad. I'm embarrassed, maybe. Which is worse."

He exhaled hard, his breath rising between us. "You shouldn't be."

"Well," I said, forcing a dry laugh, "too late for that."

The silence stretched, and for once, he didn't fill it. He didn't try to joke or explain. He just watched me, shoulders stiff under his coat.

"I know I messed up," he said eventually. "And I know it probably would've been easier to let things cool down. Give it space."

"Yeah," I murmured, stepping back. "That's what I thought we were doing."

He nodded slowly. "Maybe we still should. But... before we do..."

He looked at me—really looked at me as if there was something behind his words he didn't quite know how to shape.

"I want to show you something," he said quietly. "If you'll let me."

"Noah." I sighed, dragging a hand over my scarf, my fingers numb from more than just the cold. "You don't get to ghost me mid-heart-to-heart then show up outside my job like you're delivering redemption in a pickup truck."

"I'm not—" he started.

I cut him off with a look that said I was tired and freezing and had enough of mixed signals.

He shifted his weight like the truth made him uncomfortable.

"I'm not here to fix it all in one night," he said after a beat. "I just didn't want the last thing between us to be... that."

"That," I echoed, my lips flattening, "You mean the moment you leaned and then backed off like you imagined the whole thing?"

His jaw tightened.

"I told you I'm not mad," I added. "But that doesn't mean I'm over it either."

He nodded once, his jaw ticking, and then his voice dropped and became calmer, more serious. "Okay. That's fair."

The wind picked up again, cutting through my coat like paper. I wrapped it tighter, trying to ignore the way my chest still ached just looking at him.

"Whatever you came to show me, Noah... it better not be another apology wrapped in a riddle."

His lips twitched. "It's not."

"Good," I said, stepping back toward the sidewalk but not away. "Because if I climb into that truck with you and you give me some poetic metaphor about timing or fate again, I swear I'm jumping out before we hit the first stoplight."

A ghost of a smile crossed his face.

"No metaphors," he said. "Promise."

I narrowed my eyes.

He walked around the truck, opened the passenger door, and I climbed in, arms folded, my coat buttoned up all the way up like armor.

He closed the door gently behind me, then got in on the driver's side and started the truck with a low rumble. The heater kicked on, warming the cabin with soft blasts of air, but it didn't quite reach the nerves crawling up my spine.

Noah glanced at me once, just enough to check that I had settled into the seat, then pulled off into the snow-covered street without a word.

His hand kept adjusting the radio dial even though it was off. His grip on the wheel was too tight and too deliberate.

We drove in silence. Streetlights passed by in long stretches of gold, broken only by the occasional snowflake glittering in the beams.

I glanced at him, then back at the road. "You're not planning to, like... murder me in the woods or anything, right?"

He snorted, glancing over with a deadpan expression. "Wouldn't be my style."

"Oh, right. You'd probably just make me feel all my emotions and then vanish into the blizzard again."

That drew a slight smirk, but he said nothing further.

We turned off the main road, tires crunching over fresh snow. The street narrowed, and the tall trees cast long shadows across the hood. I leaned closer to the window, squinting at the dark shapes beyond the headlights.

He pulled onto a smaller path—barely wide enough for the truck—and the tires thudded gently over patches of packed snow. Trees closed in around us like a Christmas card from hell was swallowing us. The truck slowed, tires crunching up a small driveway.

A single porch light glowed ahead, casting soft light onto the snow-covered steps.

He parked and put the truck in park. I turned toward him slowly, eyebrows lifted. "Your house?" I asked.

He nodded, still not looking at me. "Yeah."

"The hell?" I said.

Noah finally met my gaze, a slow exhale leaving him as he reached for the door handle. He met my eyes again, sighing as if he'd been holding his breath since I climbed into the truck. "Come inside, Imara," he said.

"That sounded exactly like the setup to a horror movie," I muttered, unbuckling my seatbelt anyway. "Girl gets in a truck with an attractive, sad man. The girl gets murdered. Headlines write themselves."

Outside, the wind hit me again, but curiosity—or maybe sheer pettiness—muted it this time. I stepped out slowly, watching Noah move ahead and climb the porch as if it were the most casual thing in the world.

His porch was wide with clean steps. A solid front door painted a deep navy and flanked by potted plants that were currently buried under snow but clearly cared for overlooked the neatly shoveled driveway that looked done to ruler precision. It didn't match the quiet, humble image I had of him.

He unlocked the door and stepped aside, holding it open with no smile, no coaxing, just a small nod that said, "Your move."

I crossed the threshold slowly, half-expecting something to feel off. It didn't.

Inside, it was warm. Not just heated—but warm and lived in. A wide living room greeted me, with hardwood floors and a soft area rug that didn't match the couch but somehow worked. A coffee table sat stacked with two books, a half-burned candle, and what looked like a crossword book. A record player sat in the corner, and a blanket was thrown over the arm of the couch.

And the pictures. They were everywhere: on the bookshelf, along the hallway wall, tucked into the corners of the mirror above the console table. Mrs. Carter smiled from half of them, her arm always looped around Noah's or resting on his shoulder. There was a picture of a woman I didn't recognize, but she was young, pretty, laughing, and standing beside Mrs. Carter and him in a photo that looked older than the others.

It hit me a little harder than it should have. This place... it was his. Not just a bachelor pad, not some dark man cave where socks lived under couches and pizza boxes told stories. It was... him. Except him with pieces of her. Of them. Of who he used to be.

He shut the door behind me, and for once, I had nothing to say. He headed toward the kitchen, paused with one hand on the fridge handle, and glanced over his shoulder. "Do you want something to drink?"

I shook my head quickly. "No, I'm good." (Which was code for: No, because I was already spiraling and didn't need to add hydration-induced anxiety on top of it.)

He nodded once, then walked past me and headed straight toward the stairs.

And I froze.

He stopped halfway up, turned around, and gave me a look. "It's strictly PG-13, Imara," he said, his mouth twitching. "Scout's honor."

I folded my arms across my chest and squinted up at him. "I'd hope the Boy Scouts taught you all better than to lure women upstairs in the middle of a blizzard."

That earned me a quiet chuckle that rumbled low. I sighed—loudly, dramatically, and on-brand—and followed him up.

At the top, the hall was short and clean—walls painted a soft gray and a runner rug that looked brand new. I saw a closed door on the left, probably the bathroom and another cracked open across from it, revealing shelves stacked neatly with folded towels and what looked like extra blankets—a linen closet.

He pushed open the last door at the end of the hall, and that one was his.

His room was clean. Spacious, too. Light gray walls, a navy comforter smoothed down perfectly, a desk tucked neatly into the corner with the laptop closed, and a single framed photo of Mrs. Carter on the dresser, standing proudly in front of the café's old sign.

I hovered near the doorway, unsure for a second, then perched gingerly on the edge of the bed when he nodded.

Noah crouched beside the nightstand and pulled out a cedar chest that looked older than anything else in the room. The lid creaked softly as he opened it.

He didn't say anything. He just shifted the chest between us and started passing me photos, one at a time.

The first showed a little boy—maybe four or five—staring wide-eyed at the camera. His haircut was a little uneven, as if someone had done it in a rush. His expression was all nerves and no smile.

The next picture showed an older child—maybe six or seven—with scraped knees, sitting cross-legged on a rust-colored mat with a few other kids I didn't recognize. They weren't smiling either.

Then came another photo: Noah again, holding a plastic toy and wearing a lopsided paper crown. Behind him, a woman in scrubs rested her hands lightly on his shoulders. Her face looked kind—but not warm.

I glanced at the background—linoleum floors, beige walls, one of those plastic chairs with metal legs in the corner, and a flickering fluorescent light overhead.

I didn't need him to explain. It was an orphanage.

He still didn't speak. He just handed me another photo. And another. The process became a quiet ritual as if he were letting me into something he'd never allowed anyone to see—each photo a piece he had held onto, not because it was good, but because it was his.

Stacks of them lay there: glossy, faded, all sorted with the kind of care people use when they hold on to memories instead of people.

I glanced up at him; something heavy pressed against my chest.

He wasn't looking at me. His fingers trailed over the edge of the next photo, slower this time. He didn't hand me another photo.

Instead, he leaned back a little on his palms, staring into the box.

"You know," he began, his voice low and thoughtful, "I didn't like sweets when I was a kid."

My eyes flicked up to his face, searching. "You? Mr. Muffin Man? Pie Whisperer? You baked like it was a love language."

He gave a soft huff—half laugh, half exhale—and looked down at one of the photos in his lap. "I didn't trust them. I thought they were bribes, something people used to get you to behave, forget something, or shut up. It wasn't until I realized that the only thing that ever made the adults leave me alone was being quiet with a cookie in my hand that I started keeping them close."

My brows pulled together, but I didn't speak—not yet.

He shifted and pulled out a Polaroid. In it, he wore a faded sweatshirt that was too big for his frame, sitting at a cafeteria table with a single oatmeal raisin cookie in his hand.

"That was the deal," he said, tapping the corner of the photo with his thumb. "I figured out how to stay out of trouble, fly under the radar, be helpful, and quiet. I learned to bake something if you want people to like you. It worked. People liked sweet things—even if they didn't like you."

"I wasn't the worst kid there," he added, as if it mattered. "But I had a mouth. Questions. Anger. That kind of thing got you passed over again and again."

I watched him quietly, holding the photo he gave me as if it might slip through my fingers if I breathed too hard.

He finally looked up at me. "You ever notice I only talk about my grandma?" he asked. I nodded gently.

"She was the first one who didn't expect me to perform," he said. "She didn't care if I was useful or polite or knew how to make pie crust. She just saw me."

There was a long pause after that. He didn't fill it; he just let it sit between us like something sacred.

Almost reluctantly, he leaned forward and rested his elbows on his knees, rubbing his hands together as if trying to warm or calm himself down.

"I know you probably don't think it," he said, "but I didn't grow up in a place that taught you to believe in happy endings. And I know how it sounds, coming from the guy who owns a café and bakes muffins for a living, but that's the part people like—that's the part they take pictures of. Not the part where I stand in a room full of people who say they care and still leave."

I felt something shift in my chest.

He swallowed and finally glanced over at me again. "You're good, Imara. Better than me."

I opened my mouth, ready to shoot that down with a sharp, "Please, don't do that," but he kept going.

"And I know you don't like hearing it, but it's what I see. I didn't come from a place that taught you how to love someone without holding something back."

"I burned three trays of croissants this morning because I kept replaying that night in my head. All day at the bakery, I couldn't focus. I couldn't shut it off."

His hand tightened into a fist in his lap.

"And what messed me up the most wasn't even wanting to kiss you. It was thinking you might believe I didn't want to. That you'd think it was about you. That you'd think I didn't care. Imara, you deserve somebody who isn't still working out how to be whole. You deserve someone who can love you properly."

He didn't look away this time; he just waited, as if part of him hoped I'd run—that maybe if I did, he'd prove himself right.

I sat there, one hand still resting on the chest's lid, the other curled loosely in my lap. My thoughts were spinning.

"Noah," I said quietly, and when he glanced over, I met his eyes. "I wasn't asking you to love me."

His gaze didn't flinch, but something behind it shifted—as if he hadn't expected that or as if part of him was already bracing for the weight of more.

"We weren't even there," I continued, my voice calm, not rushed. "We were so far from that. I wasn't asking anything from you. Not really. I wasn't trying to corner you into promises or tell you what you felt wasn't valid."

I breathed in slowly.

"I just... liked being around you. That was it. You made me feel like myself again. Not someone's ex. Not a statistic or some woman limping through a heartbreak no one ever taught her how to survive. Just... me. And I didn't think I realized how much I missed that."

His brows tugged, his jaw working as if he were trying not to react, but I saw the way his hands stilled and his posture softened just a little.

"I didn't expect you to perform," I said, my tone gentler now. "From day one, you were the man who almost stole the last cinnamon but gave it to me anyway for a dinner you didn't owe me while owning an entire café. So let's not pretend like you didn't have a heart just because it had a few dents."

He huffed a short laugh and shook his head.

"We all have our ways of coping," I went on. "You bake. I overthink. Neither of us is perfect. But that doesn't mean we don't deserve to experience people, enjoy someone's company, or feel something that didn't come with a price tag."

I didn't move toward him. I didn't need to.

I just sat there, offering what I could—my honesty, my steadiness, my truth—and let it land where it would.

"It didn't have to be anything," I said finally. "It just... was. And that was okay."

He leaned forward, elbows on his knees, staring out at nothing.

"Damn," he muttered, rubbing the back of his neck. "I sounded like some sad, off-brand Shakespeare monologue over something that wasn't even that deep."

"I said it softly," I replied softly, reaching out before I could second-guess myself. My fingers curled around his forearm, which felt warm and solid beneath my touch. "It was that deep."

He finally looked at me.

"I needed to hear it," I added. "And I think you needed to say it. That mattered."

His gaze flicked to where my hand rested on his arm, but he didn't pull away.

"We've said a lot tonight," I murmured, my thumb brushing once over the fabric of his sleeve. "Maybe now... we got to learn the better parts. The ones that aren't as bruised."

His eyes fell to my mouth, and mine did the same.

And suddenly, the space between us felt fragile again, full of what-ifs, almosts, and something simmering so close to the surface it might have broken through with just one breath too close.

His fingers twitched against the comforter, just shy of mine. We were both perched at the edge of the bed, shoulders almost touching, knees nearly brushing. Not close, but not far either.

I glanced down at our hands—his inching closer without realizing, mine already halfway there. We weren't touching, but we were thinking about it. Hard.

The air shifted, warm and quiet and full of everything neither of us could say out loud.

He was watching me then—not just my face, but everything: my breathing, the tilt of my head, the tremble I tried to hide in my hand. And I let him keep watching me because I was watching too. I was reading the same unsaid language in the line of his jaw, the rise of his chest, and the way he looked at me like I was something fragile he was afraid to want too much.

His gaze dipped again—to my mouth—and that was all it took.

The moment bent.

I leaned in, just barely.

He met me halfway.

Our lips hovered so close I could taste the warmth of his breath. My heartbeat stumbled once, then took off in a sprint. The room quieted—the hum of the heater, the weight of the bed, even the ache we'd both been carrying. Everything faded.

And then his mouth brushed mine.

Soft. Careful. As if he were asking a question.

I answered without a word.

His hands found my jaw, then slid up until his palms cradled each side of my face. His thumbs rested just beneath my ears, holding me in place as he deepened the kiss, his lips moving against mine with a quiet reverence that made my whole body light up.

I went completely, stupidly breathless. I didn't even realize how dizzy I felt until I had to steady myself by leaning into his touch like it was the only thing anchoring me.

But when his mouth slanted against mine again, just a little more urgently that time, I pulled back—barely, just enough.

He stilled instantly, his forehead brushing mine, his breathing unsteady.

I was smiling—soft and a little sheepish—as I turned my head to the side and whispered, "Obviously... we aren't there yet either."

A low groan escaped him, drawn straight from his chest. "You are killing me."

I laughed genuinely and nudged his shoulder as he leaned back, his hands dropping from my skin—but only because he had to.

Noah ran a hand down his face, looking up at the ceiling for a second before huffing out a slow, amused breath. "Alright," he said, his voice still gravelly, "let's get you home before I forget I am trying to be a gentleman."

CHAPTER 15: WELL DONE

The heater was still running and humming low as he pulled into my driveway. Outside, the snow had piled high along the curb—untouched except for the tracks his truck had just made. I didn't overthink it. Whatever was between us, whatever it was becoming, I let it breathe. I didn't poke, label, or shove it into a box it wasn't ready for. I just let it exist.

"Okay, first of all," I said, pointing a gloved finger at him, "you lied. You said you'd been ice fishing dozens of times."

"I didn't lie," Noah replied, calm as ever, one hand lazily on the wheel, the other resting as if it belonged on my thigh—which, unfortunately for my brain, it sort of did now. "I said I'd been ice fishing. I never said I was good at it."

"You fell into a frozen lake, Noah."

"And yet," he said, glancing at me with that trademark slow smirk, "Here I am. Alive. Stronger. Wiser. Slightly wetter."

I snorted. "I had to fish you out."

He shrugged with absolutely no shame. "Romantic."

"It was humiliating. For me. Because you panicked and screamed like—"

"I didn't scream."

I whipped my head toward him, eyebrows shooting up. "You definitely screamed."

He looked at me as though I'd just accused him of war crimes. "I did not scream."

"Noah, you let out a sound that startled birds. In winter."

"That was not a scream. That was—" He gestured vaguely. "A surprised exhale. Maybe a manly yelp at most."

"A yelp? Oh my God."

He pulled the truck into park, leaving the engine running and the heater humming low. His hand was still warm on my leg, his thumb now drawing maddeningly slow circles as if he knew I was too flustered to fight properly.

"I'm serious," he said, smug as hell. "There was no scream. You're exaggerating."

I leaned back, crossing my arms. "You flailed."

"I lunged."

"You flailed. There were limbs. You sounded like a cartoon character falling off a cliff."

He was grinning now, wide and completely unrepentant. "I didn't even fall in. Barely got wet."

"You fell through the ice, Noah."

He pointed at himself. "And yet, I stayed dry and warm—and still breathtakingly handsome."

I let out a long, suffering sigh, mostly to hide the fact that I was smiling because I was—a lot.

"You screamed," I said again, softer now, just to needle him.

He leaned in a little, his breath warm, his smile almost unfair. "Say it one more time."

"You. Screamed."

I turned, all smug and satisfied, laughing to myself as I popped the door open. "I can't believe I forgot to tell the girls. Just wa—"

Thunk.

Something cold and wet smacked me dead center between my shoulder blades. My laughter cut off mid-breath as snow trickled down the back of my coat like betrayal—actual betrayal. I turned slowly. So slowly.

Noah was standing outside his truck now, his glove still dusted with snow, eyes wide in faux innocence. His mouth twitched as if he were trying not to laugh, but his dimples already gave him away.

"You did not just snowball me."

He shrugged, grinning like a man without regrets. "You looked like you needed to loosen up."

I scooped up a handful of snow without breaking eye contact. Game on. The snow was light and fluffy but still firm enough to pack. I threw one—it missed. He ducked behind the truck and came up laughing. I ran, slipping once and catching myself against the mailbox. He pelted me again, and I shrieked like I was in a horror movie.

"You're going down!" I yelled, laughing so hard I could barely aim.

I couldn't even see straight from laughing; my breath fogged up in front of me, cheeks flushed and soaked. We crashed into each other near the edge of my yard, tumbling into the snowbank like a pair of uncoordinated toddlers.

I landed halfway on top of him, my coat tangled in his, snow clinging to the ends of my hair and the tips of his curls. His face was flushed, his lips red from the cold, and we were both panting, grinning, completely breathless.

I braced myself on his chest to push up, but I didn't move right away. The laughter faded into something quieter and deeper. His eyes flicked to my mouth, and mine did the same. No more 'almosts.'

I leaned in first—because I could because I wanted to—and he met me without hesitation.

The kiss was warm, even with snow stuck in our hair and our noses half-numb from the cold. It started soft, easy—just a press of lips, just this. His hand found my waist. My fingers curled into the collar of his coat.

"HEY!"

We both jumped, scrambling apart as if someone had caught us doing something illegal.

"THIS AIN'T NO PARK!" our neighbor shouted from his porch, his robe billowing in the wind, a half-eaten TV dinner in one hand.

"Sorry, Mr. Ellis!" I called back, trying not to choke on my laughter as I helped Noah up.

"You got three minutes to clear off my grass, or I'm calling the HOA!"

"We don't even have an HOA!" Noah yelled back, brushing snow from his jacket, his eyes dancing.

"You talkin' back to me, boy?!"

Mr. Ellis slammed his storm door so hard it rattled in its frame. From the other side of the glass, we heard him muttering about "snow devils" and "reckless porch romancers" as if we had personally offended the sanctity of his postage-stamp lawn.

Noah looked at me. I looked at him before we both dissolved into laughter.

"I guess I'm on shovel duty," he said, resigned as he headed toward the snow pile by the porch with a mock bow. "Enjoy your warm, dry, not-in-trouble status."

"Oh, I will," I called sweetly, already peeling off my gloves. "Thanks for taking one for the team, boy."

He shot me a look over his shoulder that said, "You're lucky I like you," and I responded by sticking out my tongue through the kitchen window ten minutes later while I stirred the tea.

He paused, grinned, and then shook his head, dramatically digging deeper into Mr. Ellis's precious sidewalk.

I carried the mugs over to the table, watching him from the warmth of my kitchen. His jacket was damp, the faded pattern peeking from under his beanie, his cheeks flushed from the cold. He looked good—and still smug about beating me in a snowball fight I clearly had no business entering.

By the time he was done, he came in, stomping the snow from his boots, still laughing as he shed his coat.

"You good out there, champ?" I teased, handing him his mug.

"I was threatened, actually," he said. "So no, not really."

I rolled my eyes and took a sip. "You're fine. You've still got your dignity."

I passed him the tea with a grin, but he didn't sit as he usually did. He just wrapped his hands around the mug, soaking in the warmth a second too long before setting it back down.

"I can't stay tonight," he said in a low voice. "Ma's home. I told her I'd check in before she went to bed."

"Oh." I nodded, trying not to let a flicker of disappointment show on my face. "Of course. That makes sense."

He stepped closer, leaned in, and softly kissed my forehead. "I'll text you," he murmured, "or call—whatever you want."

My eyes fluttered closed for a moment as I soaked it in. When I looked up, Noah was still there.

"I'll be fine," I said with a soft smile, trying to ease the guilt in his eyes. "I'm just a few giggles away from sleep."

He smiled, then took my hand; his fingers wrapped around mine, grounding me. His eyes held mine as if he were trying to memorize something. "I'll see you soon," he said quietly.

I nodded. "I know."

He held onto my hand just a beat longer than necessary before letting it go. The door clicked shut behind him, and I stood there like a dork for a full ten seconds before turning back inside.

I curled up on the couch with the last of the tea, cheeks warm and insides buzzing, and eventually made my way to bed, still smiling as if the boy I'd had a crush on in high school had kissed me—because, apparently, I did.

I didn't even bother trying to sleep before I opened the group chat.

Imara:

"He kissed my forehead and told me he'd call or text—'whatever I want'—and I didn't know if I was supposed to sob, scream, or just marry him right then."

Imara:

"He also held my hand and said, 'I'll see you soon,' while looking into my soul. So if I disappear tomorrow, it's because I've melted into a puddle of feelings."

I tossed the phone aside, breathlessly laughing into my pillow, and finally let myself feel happy.

Linda:

"First of all, I would just like to thank the Lord that this man has finally acted like he has sense. Second of all, if he ever makes you cry for the wrong reason, I'm baking a casserole and hitting him with it."

Caroline:

"I KNEW IT—I KNEW HIS AURA SHIFTED. Girl, you are glowing through the phone, aren't you?"

Linda:

"Caroline, half of the time, I honestly didn't know what you were saying."

Caroline:

"Okay, your Prince Charming is behaving, but Beau's been acting weird all day. He barely spoke at lunch and then went out to the barn for about three hours. A couple of his animals didn't make it through the storm."

Imara:

"Oh no…"

Linda:

"That explains it. The man was basically a Disney prince. He probably sang them lullabies." Caroline said she was giving him space, but she felt so helpless.

Charlotte replied that they'd check in on him that weekend with cocoa, the emotional support squad, and all that. I smiled softly at the screen. Those women were pure chaos, heart, and home; even when I was sorting through my mess, I never felt alone.

Charlotte then wrote, "Let's go over there tomorrow."

Caroline responded, "Yes! We'll bring stuff. Distraction and support squad activated."

Linda added, "I'll print some pictures of his animals—the good ones. The ones where the goats looked majestic."

I typed, "I'll bring food. Something warm."

Next, Charlotte messaged, "I've got a new deck of cards. We can play something old-school."

Caroline chimed in, "I'll bake. And maybe find one of those ridiculous Pinterest 'thinking of you' baskets. He can roll his eyes all he wants. It's happening."

Linda capped it off: "10 AM. Pack your empathy and an elastic waistband. We're going in."

I smiled so wide it hurt a little, and as I pulled the blanket up and let my eyes close, I thought… maybe we were all getting better at letting people in. In our ways. In our own time.

The group chat finally quieted down just after midnight. I sent one last message confirming the food I'd bring in the morning, then plugged in my phone and slid it onto the nightstand.

But just as I was about to roll over, my screen lit up again.

Noah wrote:

"Look who's terrorizing me before bedtime."

[A photo was attached: it showed him on the couch beside Mrs. Carter, who looked like she was mid-swat—probably threatening him with something off-screen. His smile was tired but soft; she was glaring, yet her hand rested right on his knee.]

Then Noah added:

"She says she doesn't miss you, which is a lie. She asked about your banana bread twice. Also... I miss you."

I stared at the screen a second too long, my heart pounding in my chest as if it didn't know how to behave. Not a novel. Not a poem. Just three words:

"I miss you."

I bit my lip, reread the message thrice, and then set the phone down as if it might explode if I looked at it again.

I didn't know where this was going, but I was starting to hope it was somewhere good.

CHAPTER 16: OVERHEATING

By nine a.m., I was already sweating through my scrubs. Emergency codes before coffee should have been illegal— not just frowned upon, but illegal. I was still half-running on the adrenaline of the morning call, my hair barely pinned back, and my curls were fighting for their lives. My scalp was damp, my edges were traitors, and I was about two degrees away from steam rising off me like a busted kettle.

Mr. Timothy Barnes was in his late 60s, a former mechanic, and a three-time heart attack survivor. He had come in wheezing that morning and turned blue for five terrifying seconds.

"So," he wheezed with a half-smile, "if I flatlined again, would you be the one rescuing me, sweetheart?"

I stared down at him, unblinking. "Mr. Barnes, you were two inches from meeting the Lord this morning."

He shrugged, completely unbothered. "Well, he didn't seem ready for me, and I wasn't about to go anywhere without dessert."

"I don't think heaven has bread pudding," I muttered, adjusting his IV drip.

"That's hell then," he said, nodding solemnly.

I exhaled through my nose, composed myself, and tried to keep the interaction professional and grounded in the facts. But it was hard when my patient kept cracking jokes as if it were open mic night rather than the cardiac unit. I tugged the blanket a little higher over his chest. "You keep joking, but something is bothering you. I can feel it."

He didn't answer right away. The corners of his mouth twitched, and his humor faltered, but he pulled it back as if it owed him rent.

"I am fine, darlin'. Just tired," he said.

"Mr. Barnes," I said gently as I set the chart aside, "you don't have to do the tough guy thing with me. No matter what's weighing on you, it is okay to talk about it."

He looked over, his eyes crinkling at the corners—not from laughter this time.

"Now that was a tone," he murmured. "Do you talk to all your patients like that or just the ones who nearly check out before breakfast?"

"I save it for the special cases," I replied, soft but steady. "The ones who make me skip my coffee."

He chuckled, but it was thin and worn.

I pulled the stool closer. "Seriously. I am not just here to count your breaths and reset your pillows. If something was going on—anything—I am listening."

I thought I had cracked it for a moment because his jaw shifted and his hands clenched, then unclenched beneath the blanket. And his eyes—God, those eyes—turned glassy just for a second as if he might have let something slip through. He cleared his throat.

"My pops always said that a man's sorrow should be his secret. He said if you carried it long enough, it would quiet down on its own."

He gave me a tired smile. "I am alright, nurse," he said.

I nodded, even though I didn't believe it. My heart tugged somewhere beneath my badge, and I lingered at the doorway a second longer than I needed to linger before slipping out.

An hour later, I found Caroline in the break room, elbow-deep in a vending machine mystery snack—the kind that swore it was trail mix but looked like betrayal. She eyed me over the crinkle of plastic.

"You look like you have just lost a game of emotional poker," she said.

"Mr. Barnes," I said, flopping into the chair beside her as if my bones had given up.

"Ah," she said, nodding. "Tough nut."

"Tough everything," I muttered, tugging my sleeves down. "He came in the morning wheezing. I barely got him stable before he turned blue—blue, Caroline. I thought we were going to lose him right there. But he bounced back. He cracked a joke while I was still shaking. Then..."

I paused and sighed.

"Then he threw up the invisible wall and pulled a sad quote from his dad about men and secrets—as if it were gospel. He said he was "just tired.""

Caroline clicked her tongue, already scrolling through her mental Rolodex of patient-strategy techniques. "Wanna tag me in? Give me a shift with him, and I'll see if I can work my magic," she said.

"Only if you promise not to ask if he is emotionally constipated," I said.

"No promises," she sang. "But I will be subtle," she concluded.

I smirked, grateful. I knew Caroline's version of subtle usually involved card games, passive-aggressive muffins, and patients accidentally spilling their whole life story while trying to win at Uno. Whatever worked.

I was halfway through scanning Mr. Howard's chart when I heard the unmistakable shuffle of boots I had come to recognize as second nature—the kind of stride that was calm on the surface, yet quicker than it should have been, with concern pushing its rhythm.

Noah.

I looked up, and indeed—there he was. His jacket was half-zipped, snow still clinging to his hair, his brow furrowed as if he had sprinted through a storm and forgotten to breathe. His eyes landed on me, and something in them loosened.

"She's okay," he said before I could even ask. "Ma. I brought her in because she wouldn't wake up this morning and wouldn't open her eyes or answer."

My stomach dropped. "What happened?" I asked.

"She scared the hell out of me; that's what happened," he said, running a hand down his face. "I was shaking her, calling her name, thinking the worst—only for her to pop one eye open and mutter that she was resting and I needed to stop flailing like a damn trout."

I exhaled hard, one hand pressed to my chest. "Oh my God," I murmured.

"She said—and I quote—'the older I got, the deeper I had to sleep if I was going to keep this face presentable,'" he said while gesturing vaguely toward his face, deadpan.

He looked up at me, his eyes still rimmed with that earlier panic, even though he was trying to play it cool then. I crossed the space between us and sat beside him, our knees brushing ever so slightly.

"She's okay," I reminded him. "And you did the right thing. You got her here."

He nodded, but his fingers still flexed against his jeans like he was trying to shake off the leftover fear.

"She's the strong one," he said after a beat. "I just... forgot that she is also old. And human. And—"

"And still capable of scaring you senseless," I offered gently.

A breath huffed out of him—a half-laugh, half-sigh.

"Exactly that," he said.

A beat passed, and then he shifted closer, his thigh brushing against mine, his shoulder almost—but not quite—resting against me. He leaned back as if he were relaxing now that the fear was wearing off, but I could feel the shift and how his whole body softened when he was next to me.

"So..." he drawled, turning just enough for our eyes to meet. "How is my favorite nurse?"

My lips twitched. "She is surviving. She has four hours of sleep and coffee in her veins but is still sweating from almost losing a patient."

He chuckled, the sound low and warm. "Bet she still looked good doing it."

"Flattery," I said, feigning a sigh. "Predictable."

"Accurate," he murmured. "What are you doing later?"

I glanced at him, amused. "That depends. Is it a hypothetical later? Or are you about to bribe me with pie again?"

His grin spread slowly. "Bribery is still on the table. But I was thinking... maybe a little dinner? Nothing fancy. My place. Just us. No snow, no near-death fishing trips."

I smiled, genuinely and fully, and nodded before I could overthink it. "Sounds good.

He watched me for a second longer as if he wanted to say something else, perhaps something bigger. Instead, he just reached up and brushed a bit of lint off my shoulder. As easily as breathing, he leaned in and pressed a kiss to my temple.

My heart didn't know what to do with itself or with the quiet way he always made space for me, not with the way he smelled like fresh snow and coffee, not with the way I was still holding my breath when he stood.

"Text me when you're off," he said softly.

I nodded, a little dazed. "Yeah, I will."

He walked away, and I was still warm in my skin, still holding the echo of his touch like a secret, when Dr. Whitaker stepped into the hallway.

I straightened immediately.

Noah sensed it, even from a few paces away. He glanced back once. He didn't ask. He didn't call it out. He just tucked his hands into his pockets, gave me the barest smile, and disappeared around the corner.

Dr. Whitaker walked toward me, and suddenly, I was very aware of every choice I'd made that week.

"Can we talk?" he asked, his voice low. "Just for a minute."

I glanced around. The nurses' station was quieter than usual; there were no beeping machines, chatter, or sudden emergencies pulling me in five directions at once.

"Yeah," I said, quieter than I meant, "of course."

He gestured for me to follow, and we walked a short stretch of hallway until we reached one of the unused consult rooms. It was dim inside, the overhead light flickering faintly before it settled.

He didn't sit, nor did I. Something about the air—thick with whatever he was holding back—made the silence more tense than awkward.

He stood with his hands in his coat pockets, his eyes flicking briefly to mine, then past me as if he were still deciding how much to say.

"I know what you told me before," he added, his gaze sharpening slightly. "That you and Noah were just friends. That nothing was going on."

I swallowed.

"We were," I said a little too quickly. "We still are. I didn't know. It wasn't—"

"You don't have to explain," he cut in gently. "I am not here as your boss. Not even really as your colleague."

"Then... what is this?"

He exhaled through his nose, his eyes dropping for the first time as its weight settled in his chest, too.

"This is me speaking as someone who thought that maybe, for a moment, he had a chance."

I went still.

"I saw something in you back then," he said. "Something I still see. And I guess it just caught me off guard, watching it go somewhere else. I think I held onto the idea of us longer than I should have," he added. "But that is on me. Not you."

My mouth opened slightly, but I didn't know what to say. We had never had anything—just one soft no. But maybe to him, it had meant more. Maybe he had held onto the idea longer than I realized.

"I don't know why I wasn't good enough," he said finally—not bitterly, not with self-pity, but with the kind of quiet honesty that involuntarily tightened my chest. "But that doesn't mean I want to see you get hurt."

I flinched inwardly.

"I'm sorry," I said, and I meant it, even though I wasn't sure for what. For not feeling something I never could? For not pretending I might? For how things ended between us—if they had ever really begun?

"I get it," he said, a small smile tugging at his mouth. "Things change. People move forward. And honestly, I just hope it will turn into something good for you. That was all I had ever wanted. I just wanted to make sure that you were sure... I knew you were hurt before and have been through a lot. Are you sure that is the road you want to take?"

My chest tightened—not out of guilt, but gratitude. For the clean slate he was offering and for not making it harder.

"I know what I am doing," I added quietly.

But even as the words left my lips, they felt unsteady and lopsided, like I was trying to convince myself just as much as I was trying to convince him.

Did I? Because some days it felt like my heart was rebuilding itself with duct tape and denial. It felt as though I was holding too many things in my hands and pretending none were fragile. And Noah—whatever he was to me, whatever that became—was starting to feel like something I could no longer pretend away.

Dr. Whitaker nodded once—not in agreement, but with acknowledgment. Then he tucked his hands back into his pockets, stepped past me with a quiet "Take care, Imara," and disappeared around the corner.

CHAPTER 17: GOOSEBUMPS

I was standing on the wobbliest chair in my apartment—one I had told multiple people I was going to throw out "next week" for the last few weeks—with my arms stretched at full capacity, trying to wrestle the living room curtain rod back into place after it had unhooked itself as if it were tired of doing its job.

I should have just waited—for a stool, a miracle, a taller friend, literally anything other than what I did, which was to go full Final Destination by standing on tiptoe on one leg, tongue sticking out in deep concentration as if that could help gravity forget I existed.

I jolted at the sound of a loud knock and flailed, grabbing the curtain as I went, yanking the entire thing down with me in a tangle of cheap linen, knotted limbs, and what I was pretty sure was an ow-level crack from my elbow hitting the floor.

"Imara?"

The door swung open just in time for Noah to find me mid-flop, flat on my back, with the curtain tangled around my legs. He stepped in, eyes wide, the bag still in his hand, looking like he hadn't expected to find me resembling a pile of laundry. We stared at each other.

"Hey."

There was a beat.

"Did you just break your house?"

"No," I said quickly, then glanced up at the traitorous curtain rod still dangling from one side as if it were judging me. "Okay, maybe a little." He set the bag down slowly as if I might try to fall again.

"I knocked."

"I heard," I said, still lying there because, honestly, getting up felt like defeat. "You startled me. I lost my battle with physics and the curtain rod."

He squatted beside me, his mouth twitching as he tried hard not to laugh.

"You okay?"

"Mostly. Except my pride—it is unwell." He reached out a hand. I took it, letting him pull me to my feet as if I weren't clumsy and only mildly sweating from the adrenaline of almost dying in the name of aesthetics. Without asking, he slid one arm under my knees, the other behind my back, and lifted me.

"Okay—whoa—Noah!"

He stood at full height, holding me as if I were breakable and not slightly winded and tangled in what used to be my curtain. His brows pulled together as he studied my face, his eyes flicking down briefly to ascertain I was in one piece.

"You couldn't wait for me to come over?" I opened my mouth, closed it, and opened it again. He kept looking at me—gentle yet firm—almost as if he wasn't really mad but rather somewhere adjacent to anger.

I sighed, defeated, tugging the curtain's edge off my shoe. "I needed to distract myself."

He walked me over to the couch and set me down. Then he crouched again, resting his forearms on his knees, still watching me.

"From what?"

I shrugged one shoulder, trying to look anywhere but at the worry in his eyes. "Just... today. Stuff. Whitaker said something that got into my head. It was a little... weird."

His brow lifted. "Weird, how?"

"Weird like—unsolicited opinion weird." He hummed, waiting.

"He said..." I started, then trailed off, staring into my cup as if the tea leaves were dying to spell it out for me. "He said he hoped I wouldn't get hurt."

Noah's jaw ticked, but he didn't interrupt. He just leaned back slightly, waiting for the rest.

"He wasn't mean about it," I added quickly because I could already feel the tension rising in his shoulders. "He was actually really calm. The whole wise mentor energy thing—as if he were passing me a piece of ancient scroll wisdom I hadn't asked for."

"What did you say?" he asked.

"I told him I knew what I was doing," I snorted. "Which was a lie. Obviously."

He turned slightly, one arm draped along the back of the couch. "You didn't know what you were doing?"

"I mean, I thought I did. I was convincing myself I did. But then he said it, and suddenly I was like... do I?" I paused. "Because maybe I was just patching myself together with stubbornness and sarcasm and calling it emotional growth."

He studied me for a beat. Then, quietly, he asked, "Are you scared?"

I shook my head. "No. But it still got in. I didn't want to screw this up. Whatever this was."

He studied me for a moment, and then, so gently that I almost missed it, he reached for my free hand. He just brushed his fingers along mine—not even holding—just reminding me that he was there.

"You're not screwing it up," he said again, slower this time. "And even if you did—if you got scared, uncertain, or said something sideways—I wouldn't vanish on you. Okay?"

I nodded, barely. His thumbs brushed along my jaw. "Besides," he added, his mouth twitching, "you survived your own curtain rod today. You can survive feelings."

I laughed—quiet, breathy, surprised. "Low blow."

By the time we moved into the kitchen, the mood had shifted.

I pulled ingredients from the fridge, still in my scrubs with one pant leg rolled up and a braid half undone. He watched me quietly for a moment, then shrugged off his hoodie and joined me at the counter.

"Alright, Chef," he said, nudging my elbow. "Tell me what to do."

"You're on chopping duty," I declared, handing him the cutting board and pointing toward the peppers as if I meant business. "I'd do it myself, but you're the one with the good wrist-to-knife ratio."

"Is that a real thing?"

"Absolutely not," I said. "But it sounded convincing, didn't it?"

He chuckled low in his throat and started chopping while I stirred the skillet, rambling before I could stop myself.

"So, tomorrow we plan to check in on Beau—Caroline's boyfriend? You've never met him, I don't think. He runs a little farm just outside of town. A few of his animals didn't make it through the last storm, and he's been a little off since, so tomorrow, the girls and I are going. You know, for moral support. For food. Maybe an unsolicited group hug."

He glanced at me sideways, smirking. "So you are just showing up? Unannounced?"

"Think of it as planned chaos," I said brightly.

"Does he know this is happening?"

"Technically?" I scrunched my nose. "No."

Noah laughed, leaning over to tip the chopped veggies into the pan. "The man is out there grieving his goats, and he doesn't even know that a pack of unhinged women is about to storm his yard with casseroles and emotionally charged side dishes."

"That's what I was saying," I replied, wiggling my brows. "Which is exactly why you are coming too."

He paused. "I'm sorry—what?"

I spun toward him, spoon in one hand and my best pleading expression in place. "Come with me. He'd like you. Plus, I need someone there who won't get scared when Linda starts quoting from her 'spiritually sourced' tarot deck."

Noah leaned back slightly as if he were already regretting it.

I took a step forward. "Please?"

"No."

"Please," I said again, dragging it out like a whine.

He narrowed his eyes. "Don't do the puppy eyes."

I blinked innocently. "I have no idea what you are talking about."

"Imara—"

"Too late," I sang. "You're coming. Hope you like goat-themed baked goods and vague affirmations from a woman who insists she once dated a ghost."

He groaned behind me, and I didn't even have to look to know he was shaking his head.

But he was smiling.

And so was I.

He leaned in first, just slightly—just enough that his temple grazed mine when we both exhaled in unison. His skin was warm. So was the quiet little pull in the center of my chest.

"Can I say something dumb?" he asked, his voice barely a whisper.

"Only if I get to say something dumb, too," I murmured.

He didn't move away or break the contact. He just stayed there, his forehead tilted toward mine as if that were exactly where he was supposed to end up all along.

"I like you," he said simply. "A lot more than I had planned to."

The words hit me harder than I had expected. I felt them in my knees, stomach, and in the part of me that hadn't trusted easily in a long, long time.

And still—I smiled and pressed my cheek a little closer.

"I like you too," I whispered. "Kind of terrifyingly much."

His laugh was low and warm as if he'd saved it just for me. One of his hands slid gently along my arm, not possessive—just steady. Just here.

We didn't kiss.

Not that time.

But we stayed like that for a long while, just... breathing. Side by side, shoulder to shoulder, temple to temple—letting the quiet hold us in the space between everything we were and everything we were beginning to be. And it felt—finally, fully—like something real.

CHAPTER 18: COWS

We arrived like an unscheduled parade.

Four women, all bundled up in various shades of stylish coats, had their boots sinking into the half-frozen ground as we trudged toward the wide red barn sitting at the edge of Beau's property.

It was charming in that rustic, probably smelled-of-hay-and-regret kind of way. The big sliding doors had enough cracks to let us catch a whiff of cow manure and the sound of clucking chickens swirling out like a warning bell.

Linda fanned herself dramatically. "God, was that natural or artisanal farm funk?"

"I think that's cow," I offered, lifting the pan off the peach cobbler I had brought. "Please don't step in it."

Caroline, for once, was quiet. She was clutching a small bag of supplies—snacks, a thermos, and the most unreasonably adorable scarf she'd knitted for him during her night shifts. Her eyes were fixed on the barn as if she were preparing for battle... or heartbreak.

"I haven't seen him since the snowstorm," she said softly. "I don't want to seem crazy showing up like this."

Charlotte threw an arm around her shoulders. "Babe, we are literally carrying casseroles and framed photos of dead goats. That isn't crazy. That is community."

Linda held up a laminated print of what had apparently been Beau's favorite goat—rest in peace, Miss Cluckles—and nodded solemnly. "We come bearing love."

Caroline exhaled and shoved the barn door open the rest of the way.

"Beau?" she called, her voice echoing through the rafters. "Hey, it is—it is just us! Don't panic."

The barn was dim but sunlit near the open stalls. Hay crunched underfoot, chickens scattered as we shuffled in, and the heat lamps cast a reddish glow over a few sleepy cows. A soft radio in the back was playing something twangy and low.

"Beau?" I called more confidently.

Linda swatted away a chicken that was trying to peck at her boot. "Why do they always come for me?"

"Because you dressed like a street taco," Charlotte deadpanned, adjusting her mustard-yellow scarf.

I stifled a laugh and glanced toward the road, wondering—half hoping—if Noah would actually show up. He had said he would, but men said many things and showing up to a barn full of unpredictable women and grieving livestock was not exactly a dream Saturday.

The crunch of tires over gravel echoed through the lot—a soft engine hum accompanying it.

I looked up just in time to see Noah heading our way across the muddy lot, hood up, coffee tray in hand, as if he were walking into war with caffeine as his shield.

"Wow," Linda said, peeking around a horse trailer. "Your man is punctual, and he brought offerings. I like him."

"He's not—" I started, but it was pointless. Noah was already near, handing out hot cups like a farmer Santa Claus. Even Charlotte muttered a polite thanks as she warmed her fingers around her cup.

"Hey," he said softly, offering me the last cup.

"Hey." I took it, our fingers brushing for half a second too long. "You came."

Beau's truck was parked out front.

He shrugged as if it were nothing. "You asked."

That shouldn't have been enough to make my heart trip over itself. And yet it did.

"He's here," Caroline murmured, frowning as she hovered by the stall doorway. "He has to be."

Linda leaned against a beam, sipping her drink as if it were the only thing anchoring her to reality. "Maybe he's in the house?"

"He wouldn't leave his truck," Charlotte said, her eyes scanning the loft area. "And he wouldn't let those chickens out without supervision. Remember what happened last time?"

Everyone went quiet. Even the chickens seemed to pause.

Noah spoke up gently. "Maybe... he just needs space."

Caroline turned to him, her eyes wide. "You think he is crying?"

He shrugged, his expression unreadable but kind. "Sometimes grief looks like nothing at all. Just silence. Maybe he didn't want anyone to see him fall apart."

We all went quiet again, the weight of his words sinking in. The laughter from earlier felt distant now, but it wasn't unwelcome. We had come here to remind him that he wasn't alone, even if he didn't want to come to the door.

"I don't want to push him," Caroline said softly, pulling her scarf tighter around her neck. "But I also don't want to leave without letting him know... we care."

Linda squinted toward the front porch, then suddenly straightened with purpose.

"You know what? Forget this." She shoved her coffee into Charlotte's unsuspecting hands. "We're going in."

"Linda, no," I hissed, my eyes wide.

"Yes." She was already moving, her boots squishing through the slush like a soldier on a mission.

Caroline's eyes darted between all of us, torn between logic and loyalty... for about two seconds.

"Nope. She's right," Caroline said as she adjusted the foil-wrapped casserole dish in her hands and bolted after her.

"Caroline!" Charlotte yelled, half-laughing, half-horrified. "What is wrong with you two?!"

"Oh my God," I groaned, pressing a hand to my face as they stomped up the porch steps like two women with nothing left to lose. "They're actually doing it."

The rest of us hung back, silently screaming at them through our expressions, all of us standing awkwardly between hay piles and forgotten buckets of grain. Noah raised an eyebrow at me as if to say, "These are your people?"

They were halfway up the steps when—

Thump.

Another thump.

A very distinct, decidedly not innocent noise made everyone freeze.

Linda skidded to a halt.

Caroline stopped as if she had just walked into a live wire.

Charlotte looked like she had seen a ghost.

Linda's mouth opened, then closed, then opened again. "Is that—"

Caroline didn't say a word. She didn't move. She just stared at the door, wide-eyed, her arms tightening around the Tupperware of mashed sweet potatoes as if she might crush it.

Noah cleared his throat awkwardly, suddenly fascinated by the ground.

I slowly turned to him. "You said he was grieving."

"I—I thought he was!"

She was standing there like a woman possessed—her eyes wide, jaw clenched, one nostril flaring.

Charlotte saw it first. "Oh no."

"What?" Linda asked, still mildly traumatized.

"She's gonna snap," Charlotte breathed. "Somebody grab the dish before she weaponizes it—"

Caroline let out a sound. A battle cry. A banshee wail. Something primal and fueled entirely by hurt, fury, and spiritual betrayal.

"BEAU?!"

Her voice ricocheted across the entire barn like a bomb had gone off. I dropped my head into my hands.

"BEAU ELIAS MCCOY."

Noah actually jumped. "Does she—does she know his full government name?"

"Apparently!" I hissed as we all scrambled after her.

Caroline was already halfway through the door, shoving it open. We piled in behind her, all of us yelling at once.

"Caroline, wait—"

"Let's be rational—"

"This is not the time—"

But she had gone through a full Tasmanian heartbreak tornado. She was in the house now, yelling through every room with the ferocity of a ghosted, emotionally whiplashed woman left on read.

"IF YOU AREN'T DECENT, YOU BETTER GET DECENT AND START PRAYING!"

We caught up just in time to see her standing in the middle of the rustic living room—Christmas lights still up, a deer head mounted on the wall, and the faintest squeak of something upstairs that confirmed what we already knew.

Caroline threw her arms in the air like she was Moses parting the Red Sea. "YOU GOT ANIMALS OUT HERE GRIEVING, AND YOU'RE HAVING A TWO-PERSON SLEEPOVER INSTEAD OF CHECKING YOUR PHONE?"

"Crap," Charlotte mumbled.

We heard a clatter upstairs. There was movement—possibly someone scrambling for pants.

"Caroline?" came Beau's voice, dazed, confused, and terrified.

Caroline stormed toward the stairs like she was going to summon the ancestors.

"Oh no, we aren't 'Caroline-ing' now, Beau! You better come downstairs like a grown man, or I'll march up there and drag you down myself!"

Beau finally appeared at the top of the stairs—shirtless, hair wild, one sock on and one off. He looked like a man who had just remembered he'd left the stove on in another state.

"Caroline?" he repeated, blinking hard, his eyes squinting as if maybe if he blinked enough, we would all disappear.

She pointed an accusatory finger up the stairs as if she were about to cast a spell. "Who is up there? Huh? Your cousin? Your 'coworker' from the feed store? Or let me guess—your grief counselor?"

"I—I can explain," Beau stammered, stepping down slowly, one rung at a time, as if he knew each step could trigger an outburst.

Linda whispered, "He might want to skip the steps and jump straight into an apology."

Charlotte gripped my arm like it were a flotation device.

Noah whispered low behind me, "I have never seen a man regret his life choices in real-time like this."

"Babe?" A woman, a brunette in her mid-30s, wearing his flannel, appeared at the top of the stairs. "What's going on?"

Silence.

It was pure, sharp silence—so complete you could have heard a mouse breathe.

The woman looked down at all of us: a group of frozen, wide-eyed women and one very smug, very silent man with coffee in his hand. Her brows furrowed. "Who are they?"

Beau opened his mouth, then closed it, then opened it again.

"This is... uh... Caroline. And some people I know."

Caroline's eye twitched.

The woman frowned. "I'm sorry, is this about the cows? I swear we're doing everything we can to keep them warm."

Caroline's hand flattened over her chest. "The cows?"

"Right, because of the storm," the woman said kindly as she stepped down a few stairs. "It's been a mess. Anyway, I'm Erin. Beau's wife."

Charlotte made a strangled noise that sounded like she'd just swallowed a frozen grape. Linda gasped so dramatically that it echoed. Noah stared at Beau as if he might join Caroline in the smiting.

Caroline laughed. Not a soft laugh. Not even a bitter laugh. No— Caroline involuntarily let out a sound that felt like equal parts disbelief, fury, and spiritual betrayal.

"Oh. Oh, so this—" she waved a hand between Beau and his actual wife "—this was why you ghosted me? You were out here playing Noah's Ark with farm animals and family values?!"

Erin blinked. "Wait. Ghosted?"

Caroline flashed a smile so sharp it might have drawn blood. "It's fine. I'm fine. We're fine, ladies." She turned on her heel, her coat flaring like a cape. "Let's go."

And just like that, the stampede of humiliated, emotionally burned women turned as one—shooing chickens, dodging manure, dignity trailing behind like a broken scarf in the snow.

CHAPTER 19: MOONWATER AND RAGE

There was powdered sugar everywhere: On the counters, our sleeves, and in Caroline's hair, but none of us had had the heart to tell her.

She was currently three pastries deep into an emotional spiral, alternating between sobbing, laughing, and muttering about lunar alignments and betrayal under a waxing moon.

Noah slid a tray of croissants onto the table without a word. He had seen enough unhinged girl-group drama to know that silence was survival.

"I mean—his wife," Caroline said, her voice wobbling as she wiped her nose with a napkin, then immediately used the same napkin to dust powdered sugar off her scone. "I had a whole Pinterest board for our wedding. Farmhouse chic. Goats in flower crowns. An unplugged ceremony under the stars."

"Sweetheart," Linda said, gently nudging a latte toward her, "you were about to name his chickens after your zodiac sign."

"He told me he liked moon water! What was I supposed to think?" Caroline protested.

Charlotte leaned back in her chair, arms crossed. "You were supposed to think that no man who owned one flannel and lived on a farm was ever emotionally available."

I stifled a laugh behind my mug. Noah caught my eye from behind the counter, one brow raised in that "this is your crew?" kind of way. I shrugged. These were my people.

Caroline sniffled, then perked up slightly. "I'm making a spell jar. For justice. For clarity. For men to experience period cramps."

"Add Beau's name twice," Linda said, dead serious.

Noah walked over, leaned against the table, and slid another slice of pie in front of Caroline as if he were carefully feeding a wild animal. "On the house."

Caroline wiped her eyes. "You're a good man, Noah. Too good for this broken world."

He cleared his throat, shot me a glance, and muttered, "I'm not that good."

Charlotte smirked. "And yet, somehow, you're still not married to someone else. It's funny how that works."

I shot her a look over my cup. She just shrugged, unapologetic.

Caroline lifted her latte like a toast. "To farm boys who aren't married."

"To not doing background checks on men who own goats," Linda added.

"To moon water and rage," Charlotte said, lifting her donut.

I glanced at Noah, who was watching us like we were a one-act play; he couldn't stop watching.

"To friendship," I said softly, raising my mug.

"To friendship," he echoed.

He set the dish rag down, rounded the counter, and slid into the seat next to me. Right next to me.

Our thighs brushed. Our shoulders did that thing where they almost, almost touched but didn't. His hand landed on the table, close enough to mine that I had to focus on my coffee rather than the gravitational pull of the heat radiating from his skin.

Caroline clocked it immediately. Her eyes widened.

Linda noticed next, biting the inside of her cheek to hide a smile.

Charlotte didn't bother pretending. She leaned back with her arms crossed, expression smug. "Would you look at that?" she said, gesturing vaguely between us. "Chemistry in a mug-filled café."

"Stop it," I hissed under my breath, nudging Charlotte with my foot from under the table.

Caroline sighed dramatically. "They grow up so fast."

"I swear to God," I whispered again, cheeks warming as I tried to hide behind my mug.

Noah didn't say anything. He just smiled as if this were the best entertainment he'd had all week and rested his elbow on the back of my chair—casual, easy until his fingers grazed the top of my shoulder. Barely. But enough. Enough that the girls' heads all swiveled in unison.

"All of you," I warned, "need new hobbies."

But they just laughed, sipping their drinks like they hadn't just witnessed a whole damn turning point.

Then the bell over the café door rang—a soft, innocent, harmless chime. I barely glanced up. It was probably someone picking up a to-go order or a local in dire need of an extra pie. It was a Saturday, after all.

Charlotte glanced toward the sound, her brow furrowing slightly.

Linda tilted her head. "New face."

I was only half-listening.

Something inside me started to buzz—a low thrum under my ribs, like a warning, like my body knew something before my brain could catch up. So I glanced toward the door. And I went still.

No.

No... no, no, no.

That same awful, arrogant swagger—wrapped in a too-flashy leather jacket that I had specifically told him made him look like a knockoff stunt double from a clearance-bin action movie.

Derek.

In Vermont.

He was standing in Noah's café like it was normal. Like Vermont was his town.

My blood ran cold, and my cup nearly slipped from my hand. I grabbed the table edge instead. Hard.

"Imara?" Charlotte's voice cut through the low hum of the room.

Noah's eyes flicked to mine. He read it instantly. He always did—the way I had frozen, the panic inching up my spine like cold fingers.

"Who is that?" Linda asked slowly.

Noah leaned in. "You okay?"

I forced my head to shake once—a lie and a prayer. But my mouth was dry, and my vision had tunneled, and all I could think was—

What the hell was Derek doing in Vermont?

And how had he found me?

CHAPTER 20: BLAST FROM THE PAST

Derek's eyes locked on mine as he approached, completely ignoring the tension that hummed off every woman at that table.

His smile was smug and lazy in that practiced, polished way I used to fall for. It was the same smile he had worn the first time we met and the same one I had seen in a mirror after every apology he barely meant. And now he was wearing it in my safe space.

"Imara," he said, as though my name were a gift, his voice dipped in syrup and arrogance. "Damn. You look good."

The girls all turned in sync like a flock of gossip-hungry vultures. Caroline leaned back in her chair and crossed her arms. "Well, this got interesting," she remarked. Charlotte raised her donut mid-bite and muttered, "Somebody holds my earrings."

Noah stood up before I did—slowly and controlled. His chair slid back with a whisper, but the way he stepped in front of me spoke volumes. I found my voice somewhere beneath the shock and nausea.

"…Derek?" The name slipped out before I could stop it.

Every head at the table turned hard. Caroline choked on her drink. Charlotte's jaw dropped, and Linda was halfway through pushing back her chair as if someone had just lit a fuse.

"No," Charlotte breathed. "The Derek?"

"The one who cheated on you with—" Linda started, her voice rising like a siren.

"Yes," I cut in, loud and tight. My fingers clamped around my mug until my knuckles went white. "That Derek."

Linda was already on her feet. "I'm going to pepper spray him with cinnamon sugar," she declared.

"Linda—" I began.

"No, Imara. I've got years of pent-up aggression and a purse full of vengeance," she replied.

"Linda."

Too late. She was already rounding the table like a woman with a mission and a closed-case file. I shot up and grabbed her arm, blocking her path before she could lunge. "Stop. Just—just give me a second," I pleaded.

She glared at me as if I'd betrayed the sisterhood. "You're seriously gonna talk to him?"

"I'm seriously gonna get him out of this café before we all end up in someone's mugshot montage," I muttered.

Noah hadn't moved. He stood close behind me, quiet and still, but I could feel the tension rolling off him in waves. I glanced back once at his set jaw and unreadable eyes and turned toward Derek.

"Outside. Now."

Derek raised his brows, all faux charm and old habits. "Sure. We can talk—"

I didn't give him the chance to finish. I was already walking toward the door, grabbing my coat without putting it on, and stepping into the cold because I needed space—and because whatever this was, it wasn't going to unfold in front of Noah, my girls, or the tray of cinnamon twists I suddenly couldn't bear to look at without wanting to scream.

"What are you doing here?" I demanded.

His breath fogged in front of him. "I came back for you," he said.

My eyes narrowed. "You thought I'd be back in Virginia by now?"

He nodded once, sheepish. "Yeah. I... I did."

"Unbelievable," I muttered.

He stepped forward. "I've been saving everything—for this. Every word I wanted to say. Every apology. I know it's late, but I needed to say it."

I stared at him as though I was still trying to figure out if this was a joke or just a particularly vivid nightmare. "We are over, Derek. Done. You made sure of that when you slept with my best friend and let me find out like it was just... a phase. Why would you come to Vermont, of all places? You think I'm stupid?"

His face flinched. "No. God, Imara, no," he pleaded.

"Because that's what this is, right?" My voice rose, not loud but sharp. "You show up in the middle of my life like it's a movie, and you're the leading man. Newsflash—you're not."

He exhaled slowly. For once, he didn't try to charm his way through it. "I'm not here to rewrite the past. I messed up. I messed up so badly I don't even know how you looked me in the face the day you left. But I've been alone since then. And not the kind of alone that teaches you how to move on—the kind that holds up a mirror," he confessed.

I didn't say anything.

"I left Tania," he said quietly. "Months ago. I stopped pretending what we had was anything but a mistake. I've been seeing a therapist. For real, this time. Working through the things I refused to deal with before."

My arms crossed tighter over my chest, not to protect myself from the cold but from him. "I know how crazy this is," he continued. "I know showing up like this was probably the last thing you ever wanted. But I came to fix it. If you come back with me, Imara... you won't have to carry it all anymore. No more working two jobs. No more supporting us. I'll take care of the apartment. I'll fix your car. We'll take a real vacation for once."

I blinked, stunned into silence, not because it was romantic, but because he was finally saying the right things, the very things I had used to beg him to say. Just... years too late.

He met my gaze. "I promise you. I'm ready now," he affirmed.

My jaw locked, and the ache in my chest pulsed because I remembered wanting this. I remembered wanting it so badly that it made me sick.

But now? Now I had something else. A small town. A warm café. A man who never asked me to shrink.

Once upon a time, I would have fallen apart hearing this. I would have cracked right down the middle at the sound of his voice softening—at the offer to finally fix things. I would have gone with him once because I thought fixing him meant saving me, too.

But now? I looked at Derek—really looked at him—and all I felt was disgust. Not pity. Not regret. Not even sadness. Just... done.

"You need to go home," I said, my voice steady and calm in that way that only came after the storm had already passed. "You came all this way for nothing. I've moved on."

His jaw ticked, his eyes flicking toward the café window. And I knew what he saw: Noah.

He watched from inside, his arms crossed and his unreadable expression taut across his face. My girls had clustered behind him like furious backup dancers in pastel sweaters.

Derek huffed a breath and rubbed a hand over his mouth. "It's him, isn't it?" he said.

I didn't answer because it didn't matter. Noah wasn't why I was standing there with steel in my spine. He wasn't why I had said no.

But Derek drew his own conclusion. He nodded once, slowly. "Fair enough," he said. He turned as if he were going to leave, then stopped halfway between desperate and defeated.

"I'm not well, Imara," he said, his voice dipping lower and tighter. "Not just in the poetic I'm-heartbroken way. I'm… going through some things. Back home. Stuff I couldn't exactly fix on my own."

My brow furrowed just slightly and he saw it.

"I'm not trying to guilt you," he added quickly, raising his hands. "I just… thought maybe if you had heard me out, it might have meant something. I didn't come here to beg; I came here to tell you I was trying. Even if you were done with me."

I shifted, discomfort prickling down my spine as the wind bit colder. "I am done with you," I said.

He nodded again without fighting it. He just stepped back, his eyes tired and older than I remembered. "Still won't give up," he said quietly, half to himself. "But I'll let you be for now."

He walked off without waiting for a response, and I stayed there frozen, heart pounding, and throat dry, not because I was conflicted, but because I knew he meant it. Derek wasn't done. But I was.

CHAPTER 21: COLD SHOULDER

The second I stepped out of my car, I felt the tension. It was like I had walked into a room mid-argument—except it wasn't a room at all. It was the damn hospital parking lot. And the reason?

Derek.

He was leaning against that same rental as if he were there for no reason again, probably waiting for me to acknowledge him or be the first to break. I didn't. Instead, I clenched my jaw, and apparently, that was all the signal the girls needed.

Caroline appeared at my side first, her lips set tight and her eyebrows sharp enough to slice glass. "Don't even look his way. Look this way. At me. Like we're talking about skincare or murder."

Linda popped up on my other side, clutching her coffee like it was a weapon. "I had an extra-large ready, and I wouldn't hesitate to throw it in his face if he so much as opened his mouth."

"I'm fine," I muttered, even though my shoulders were stiff and my stomach was staging a full-blown protest. "It's fine."

"He's still here, Imara," Caroline said, her voice tight. "It's not fine."

We pushed through the sliding doors like a wall of divine feminine vengeance, and the minute we hit the lobby, I exhaled a breath I didn't know I was holding. Derek didn't follow. Not today. Thank God.

My first stop was Mrs. Whitaker's room, mostly because I needed a second to breathe, but also because...I missed her. And I knew she would cut through whatever fog I had allowed to settle over my brain these past few days.

She was propped up in her chair when I walked in, her blanket folded neatly over her lap, and her expression? Frosty.

"You look tired," she said, squinting at me as if trying to X-ray my soul. "Or is that disappointment I see clinging to your edges?"

I blinked. "I—"

"Noah told me."

Ah. Of course, he did.

"He didn't give details," she added, waving one hand as if that could soften the blow, "but he didn't need to. You had that look—the one women get when the trash they took out tries to crawl back into the house."

That stung—but she wasn't wrong.

"I didn't invite him here," I said, walking over to adjust her pillow even though it didn't need adjusting. "I didn't even know he knew where I was."

She snorted. "Trash always finds a way. But you're not weak, Imara. Don't let him get in your head."

"I'm not. I just... he showed up at the café."

"The café?" Her head jerked back so fast I thought I heard her neck crack. "Oh, that boy's lucky I wasn't twenty years younger. I would have dragged him by the ear into the nearest dumpster myself."

A laugh escaped me before I could stop it.

"Please don't pop a blood vessel for me," I said, gently patting her hand.

She grabbed mine before I could pull away.

"Listen to me," she said, her voice lower now, steadier. "You've been through the kind of hurt that takes time to heal. The kind that doesn't always leave visible bruises but still makes you flinch. And that man—that boy—he doesn't get to undo your peace just because he suddenly found his conscience."

I swallowed hard.

She held my hand a beat longer, then sighed and leaned back in her chair.

"My grandson," she said, her voice shifting into something warmer, gentler, prouder, "he's blooming."

My eyebrows lifted. "Noah?"

"Mm-hmm." She nodded as if she had the tea and the receipts. "He's softer lately. Still grumpy as ever, but lighter. His tea is better, too. He no longer tosses a bag in hot water every morning and calls it a day. No! He waited, let it steep, and brought it to me in one of the good mugs."

I smiled, blinking back something suspiciously close to tears.

"He even took more pictures," she added. "Of the café, of me, of that ridiculous stray cat that wouldn't stop following him. But he notices more now. He pays attention."

She turned her gaze back to me. "He's better with you. Not because you fixed him but because you gave him something he thought he didn't deserve. And it scared him. It should have. That meant it was real."

I pressed my lips together, fighting that slow ache in my chest.

"You two," she said gently, "are good for each other. But only if you both show up like you mean it. No halfway. No disappearing. That kind of love doesn't survive in silence."

I nodded.

Because she was right.

Because I needed to hear it repeatedly until I started to believe it myself.

She squeezed my hand one last time before letting go. "Now go on. I'm not dying today, and your shift just started. I need entertainment."

I smirked, my shoulders relaxing just slightly. "Yes, ma'am."

The rest of the day passed in flashes—monitors beeping, charts being updated, Caroline popping her head into the nurse's station every hour to check on me without saying what she was doing. I got through it. Not gracefully, not without tension tugging behind my eyes, but I did.

By the time my shift ended, the sun was gone, and the air outside had grown thick with that kind of winter quiet that made you want to bury yourself in blankets and disappear.

The bell above the door rang when I walked into the café—my café.

Okay, not mine. But it was mine in all the ways that mattered. My soft landing. My laughter on long days; my comfort in the form of warm pie and better company.

But that day?

I stepped inside, brushing the snow from my coat, expecting— hoping—for that usual flicker of warmth when I saw him.

Noah was already behind the counter, sliding pastries into the display with a level of precision that said he'd been up for hours. He looked up when he heard the bell and met my eyes.

"Hey," he said, grabbing a to-go cup and punching the lid into place. "Usual?"

"Yeah," I murmured, trying to smile through the weirdness. "Thanks."

He nodded. He didn't say much else.

He moved behind the counter as if he were trying to fill the silence with action. My coffee appeared like magic. Then my little box arrived—two mini pies, with an extra one tucked in as usual. But he didn't mention it. He didn't say anything. There was no dumb joke about me keeping him in business, no teasing glare when I peeked inside to confirm the flavor. He simply wiped the counter again, even though it was already clean, and nodded to a customer waiting behind me.

I hovered for a moment before leaning in, my voice low. "Noah," I said.

He looked up—just slightly.

"I know this week's been—" I began, only for the bell to ring again. My stomach dropped; I didn't even need to turn around to know who it was. I could feel that familiar, smug heat crawling up the back of my neck like a rash I thought I'd gotten rid of.

"Black coffee," Derek said smoothly. "Anything you'd recommend, Mara?"

Noah's entire body stilled. He didn't look at me. He didn't speak. He just grabbed a cup and started pouring.

I finally turned. Derek was leaning against the counter's edge like he belonged there—as if this café was just another stop on his redemption tour.

"I actually don't think you drink coffee," I said flatly.

He smirked. "Doesn't mean I can't start," he replied.

Noah set the cup down in front of him—clean, professional, emotionless—but I could see the tension in his jaw, the tight grip on the lid. His knuckles went white.

Derek raised his cup, nodding as if he had just made a perfectly normal stop at a perfectly normal place—and not, I didn't know, crashed into my safe space like a wrecking ball with too much cologne.

"Good stuff," he lied, taking a sip and grimacing before looking at Noah. "Bitter. You always go for the strong kind?"

"I go for the real kind," Noah said evenly. "Now, unless you need anything else, we've got other customers."

Derek's eyes flickered. He leaned back against the counter slowly and measuredly. "Just being friendly. I'm new in town—figured I'd support local business," he explained.

I could practically feel Noah's staff watching from behind the bakery racks. Customers tried not to stare, and I wanted the earth to open up and swallow one of us. I wasn't picky.

I took a step forward, placing myself halfway between them.

"Noah," I started, trying to give him a lifeline, a reason not to throw a pie across the café.

But he didn't look at me. He simply stared at Derek and smiled.

"Welcome to Vermont," he said.

I tugged Derek out the café door so fast that he nearly spilled the coffee he didn't even drink.

"Okay," I said, spinning on him before he could get a word in. "Let me make this perfectly clear. We're not doing this again."

His face filled with wide-eyed confusion, as if I hadn't just walked him out before he could make things worse.

"I just wanted to talk—" he began, but

"You already talked," I cut in. "You've had your moment. I listened to the whole dramatic declaration, the reformed ex-monologue, and all of it. That was your grace period. This? This is you overstaying."

He stiffened. "Imara—"

"No. Don't 'Imara' me," I said, stepping closer and lowering my voice to a tone meant only for him. "You don't get to pop up like a ghost in places you don't belong and try to wedge yourself into a life that doesn't include you anymore."

His mouth opened, but I didn't give him the chance.

"I don't care how sincere you think you are. I don't care how many therapy sessions you paid for. I don't care if Tania ran off with your wallet and ego; we're done! You showing up is not love; it's obsession. And if you keep pushing, I swear to God, I will find out what the Vermont police do with men who can't take no for an answer," I declared.

His mouth snapped shut.

"Go home, Derek," I said, low and final. "And don't come back."

He stared at me as if I had just slapped him.

Something shifted behind his eyes—whatever mask he'd been holding together cracked at the edges. For a second, I swore he was about to say something, apologize again, beg, and plead. But then his fingers tightened around the cup in his hand—too tight.

And with one sharp, angry motion, he tossed it. It clattered against the sidewalk—coffee splashing across the slush, the lid spinning once before it settled, slow and mocking.

"You used to need me," he muttered, more to himself than to me.

I raised an eyebrow. "And now I don't," I replied.

That silenced him.

The wind picked up, biting and cold, but I didn't flinch. I just stood there, arms crossed, watching the last remnants of whatever fantasy he had built about us blow clean away.

Derek looked at me as if he was seeing me for the first time and didn't like what he saw.

He didn't say another word. He just turned, his jaw tight, fists shoved into his coat pockets, and walked back to his car like a man who had finally gotten the message.

I headed back inside, tugging my coat off with fingers still trembling from the cold—and from him.

The café smelled like cinnamon and espresso, and everything was warm, which I used to look forward to. But now the air felt heavy—and it had nothing to do with the weather.

Noah was behind the counter again, his hands flying with practiced ease. He was in the zone—taking an order, sliding a plate across the counter, calling out someone's name with a too-bright smile that didn't reach his eyes.

He didn't look at me. Not right away.

I took a step forward, fumbling for words. "Noah, I just—" I began, but he interrupted.

"Lunch hour," he said quickly, his tone not unkind but firm. "It's slammed."

I blinked. That was it? After the coffee standoff from hell? My mouth opened, then closed.

The hurt flashed faster than I could tuck it away. I nodded once and stepped back.

But then, he glanced over. His jaw softened—just a little.

"I'll come by tonight," he said, his voice lower, meant only for me. "I promise."

I swallowed the knot in my throat and nodded again.

Noah dropped the bag of popcorn on the coffee table without a word and shrugged off his jacket. I had already gotten the movie playing—something fast-paced and brainless. It was background noise, a distraction I had picked on purpose.

He settled beside me in his usual spot but didn't sink in or relax that night. He stretched one arm along the back of the couch, but it didn't touch me. His legs didn't brush against mine. There was space—measured, intentional.

I pretended not to notice.

He hadn't said much since he walked in—a quiet "Hey" at the door, nothing else; no teasing, no smart remarks about how my place still smelled like cinnamon and hospital-grade fatigue.

We sat like that through the opening scene, me with my hands curled under the blanket, him not even reaching for the popcorn.

"You okay?" I asked softly.

Noah didn't look at me right away. His jaw flexed once, then again, and he breathed out slowly.

"I don't buy it," he said.

I blinked. "Buy what?"

He finally turned to me. His gaze was steady—not hard, not cold, just steady.

"That he's here just to play nice," he explained.

I froze. The pause stretched; the movie kept playing—tires screeching, dialogue racing—but none of that mattered.

"You've been quiet," he added, his tone quieter now. "Smiling too much and making everything feel like a joke. That isn't you. Not really."

My throat tightened. "I'm not—"

"I'm not judging," he said quickly, holding up one hand as though he could stop the defenses spilling out of me. "I'm not asking for explanations. And I'm sure as hell not trying to make you choose anything. I'm just..." His fingers curled into his palm. "I'm not stupid, Imara."

I looked down at my lap. "I know you're not stupid, Noah," I replied.

He shifted again, his body angling toward mine—not closer, just present, rooted.

"You didn't have to explain him to me," he said after a beat. "But don't pretend like this wasn't messing with your head and heart."

That was the thing—I had already made my choice. Derek was just the static I hadn't quite tuned out yet.

I looked up, about to say it—about to finally say something real—but he was already watching me with that same expression I had seen a hundred times and still didn't fully know how to name.

We sat shoulder to shoulder, warm beneath the blanket, while the chaos from the movie filled the silence between us.

And maybe that was enough for now.

He didn't need words, and I didn't need to pretend.

I was staying with him.

CHAPTER 22: COMING AROUND

The bookstore was mostly empty. A retired couple lingered in the travel section, whispering over guidebooks for Greece, while the cashier at the front hummed along with the instrumental jazz playing overhead. Now and then, a floorboard creaked—just enough to remind me that this place was older than half the town.

I breathed in deeply, forcing my shoulders to relax as my fingers glided over book spines while I moved through the fiction aisle. The place had a smell I had always loved—paper, wood polish, and something faintly herbal, like someone had once spilled tea on the poetry shelf, and no one had ever bothered to clean it up properly.

I paused by a row of used thrillers and ran a thumb over the faded corner of one cover, pretending I wasn't still half-frozen inside.

"Imara?"

I turned, startled—until I saw the familiar face of Mr. Ackerman. He was in his late seventies, had come in for a heart checkup last month, and had even tried to convince me that his chest pain was "probably just too much maple syrup." He was holding a stack of Westerns in one hand and a cane in the other.

"You look tense," he said bluntly.

I blinked and then managed a small smile. "Thanks, Mr. Ackerman. I'll add it to my morning affirmations."

He grinned, tapping one of the books against his cane. "We Vermonters notice these things. You okay?"

"Yeah. Just needed a quiet place."

"Well, you picked the right one. Although I hear the knitting club in the back gets rowdy after two p.m."

I laughed softly, my shoulders easing. "I'll make sure I'm gone by then."

He nodded kindly and then shuffled off toward the nonfiction aisle, still muttering about how nobody wrote cowboy justice the way they used to.

Then, out of nowhere, a voice cut clean through my calm: "Well, if it isn't Vermont's finest nurse." I turned slowly, already knowing whose voice it was.

Derek was leaning against the end of the aisle as if he belonged there. He held a copy of Love in the Time of Cholera—of all things— and flipped through it casually. A pair of boots squeaked against the hardwood near the check-out counter, and every sound felt too loud and too quiet.

"What are you doing here?" I asked evenly.

He shrugged. "Thought I'd see what this charming little town liked to read. Maybe pick up something for the plane."

"Plane?"

"I leave next week," he said. "Maybe sooner. Just depends."

My chest tightened. Good. That was good—exactly what I wanted to hear. He didn't move away. If anything, he drifted a little closer, forcing me to shift back a step without thinking—and bump into the edge of a freestanding display. A stack of romance novels wobbled behind me; one fell with a soft thud onto the floor.

Derek paused but didn't help—instead, he just watched me as I glanced down and slowly put the book back in place.

"Figured I'd use the time to tie up loose ends," he said. "Make amends. I'm working on myself, remember?"

I gripped the edge of the display, letting my fingers press against the wood. "Try working on boundaries."

He laughed softly, tilting his head. "Still got that fire. I missed that."

The way he said it made my stomach turn as if he thought this was flirting—like it was some slow-burn reunion waiting to happen. Somewhere near the back, a kid burst into laughter, and a bell rang as someone entered, letting in a gust of cold air. I tried not to flinch or notice how my heart sped up like I was trapped, even though the door was easily accessible.

Derek's eyes never left me. "Imara," he said, quieter now, "I know you hate me. You should. But this wasn't some impulsive stunt. I meant what I said. I've been working on myself. I left Virginia to show you that."

I stared at him hard. "You left because you burned through everyone else. Don't act like this is some grand gesture."

His jaw ticked. "You really think that's what this is?"

"I think you're used to walking in and getting forgiven. And I'm not that woman anymore."

"I'm not asking you to be her," he muttered, his gaze dropping to the floor. "I'm asking for a chance to show you I've changed."

I shook my head, stepping back to let the space between us widen. "You're not here to show me anything," I said. "You're here because, for once, someone didn't chase after you. You're used to running the show and hate that someone else might have gotten there first."

His eyes snapped up at that. "That man, at the café," Derek said in a tightening tone, "at the café?"

My heart stuttered, but I didn't flinch. "So?"

Derek's mouth twisted. "So, that's what this is? You and some guy who bakes muffins for a living?"

"No," I answered calmly. "This is me finally not looking over my shoulder." (More than that.)

"I'm not leaving, Imara. Not yet. I don't care if he's perfect or if you hate me. I needed to look you in the eye and tell you that I know what I did. I know what I broke. And I still want to fix it."

I stared at him, and for once, I didn't feel shaky or overwhelmed. I felt sure.

"You can't fix it. Save the rest for your therapist."

The smile he'd been wearing slipped, if only for a second. He threw the book down on the nearest display table.

"I'm serious," I said, locking eyes with him. "Go home, Derek."

His eyes darkened. "I don't have one without you."

I adjusted my scarf, lifted my chin, and walked away, leaving him standing there with nothing but an unopened copy of a love story he would never understand.

"You should have thought about that when you still had me."

The door chimed behind me as I pushed out into the cold, but it no longer felt sharp.

I made it to my car without crying. Barely. My hands gripped the steering wheel for too long before I remembered the keys were in my coat pocket. I shoved them into the ignition, started the engine, and sat there—engine humming, heart racing, and nowhere I actually wanted to go.

He was everywhere. That was the part that drove me crazy. At the café, the hospital, and in stores I knew he never shopped at—as if he had just happened to be walking by. Smiling. Soft-voiced. Calculated.

People began to ask questions. Noah wasn't quite Noah anymore. He still texted me. He still showed up on our nights together. But something in his eyes had shifted. Something careful. Something distant.

And I hated it. I hated how I couldn't simply shake Derek off like bad perfume—how he had latched onto this town as if he had earned the right to be here, as if he had earned space in this version of my life. He hadn't.

I pulled into the hospital parking lot out of habit; even though I didn't have a shift that day, the thought of being alone still made me itch. So I sat in the staff lounge with a stale donut and a half-finished crossword puzzle, watching the second hand on the wall clock twitch forward like it was taunting me. By noon, I had filled in the same row of boxes five times. By one, I knew I couldn't keep doing that, so I pulled out my phone, stared at the screen for far too long, and finally tapped Mom's name.

After two rings, she answered.

"Hey baby!" she chirped, way too cheerfully. "It must be my lucky day—my phone actually rang, and it wasn't spam or that man trying to sell me extended car insurance."

I managed a faint smile and said nothing.

"Oh, and your Aunt Bernice sends her love, and she's still mad you didn't call her back about that peach cobbler recipe. I told her you work twelve-hour shifts saving lives, not measuring nutmeg."

Still, I kept silent.

After a moment, she continued, "I was just about to make some tea and start folding laundry. You're not calling to tell me you joined a cult or got married in secret, right? Because I felt something earlier—a flutter in my chest. I thought it might have been maternal intuition."

"Mom."

Something in my voice finally broke through her rambling, and she went silent.

"...What happened?"

I took a shaky breath. "Something's wrong."

Her tone shifted completely. Gone was the playful warmth; in its place came a sharp, focused readiness to handle it.

"Tell me."

So I told her everything: about Derek, about how he'd shown up in Vermont as if nothing had changed—like he hadn't left a crater in my life or torched every bridge on his way out. I told her about the café, the bookstore, and how I didn't exactly feel scared, not in the traditional sense—I just felt as though the air was sucked out of the world, leaving nowhere that was truly mine.

And she listened in silence until I finished. Then she said,

"That raggedy little boy had the nerve to come to Vermont?"

"Mom—" I began.

"No. No. I need to understand. He wrecked your life in Virginia, humiliated you, cheated on you with someone who dared to call herself your best friend, and now—what? He's treating your healing like it's a vacation spot?"

I winced but couldn't stop her.

"Oh, he has lost his mind," she continued, her voice growing fierce. "Showing up with that slick voice and those bargain-bin apologies like he hadn't torn your heart to pieces—and in my daughter's town? Oh, no, ma'am."

"Mom, please don't—"

"I'm serious, Imara. I'll call his mother right now. I'll drive to her house, knock on her door, and tell her, 'Come collect your embarrassment of a son before he finds out what it's like for
Page | 286

someone to pray over him while swinging at him in the same breath.'"

In the background, I heard Dad's voice: "Who is she yelling about?"

"Derek!" she hollered. "Our child just told me he's back."

"He's what now?" Dad asked, his tone growing stern. "Where is he?"

"Walking around Vermont like he didn't throw his whole future away!"

"I can drive up tonight," Dad declared, dead serious. "Got gas in the tank, a bat in the trunk, and arthritis cream in the glove compartment."

"Y'all," I groaned, pressing my fingers to my forehead. "Please don't start a riot."

"You should've told us sooner," Mom said softer now. "You don't have to carry this by yourself, baby. Not ever again."

"I didn't want to make it bigger than it was," I admitted.

"It is big," she said. "Because that boy represents everything you had to heal from. And we're not letting him set you back—not one step."

"You're doing everything right," Mom added firmly. "You moved. You rebuilt. You're loving people who love you back. That man is a footnote, Imara. And if he doesn't know it yet—he will."

Dad then got back on the line. "Tell him if he shows up again, he's got one warning. After that, I go full Old Testament."

"Dad."

"I will smite him, Imara. You know I will."

I laughed through my tears. "You're both insane."

"Okay. Now listen to me. I know you said he's just hanging around, but if you ever feel unsafe—even for a second—you call the police. Then you call us. In that order."

"I don't think he's a physical threat," I murmured. "It's not like that. He's just in my space and in my life. And it's messing with my head."

"Sweetheart," Dad said gently, "people like that—the ones who don't respect a 'no'—don't always announce themselves loudly. Sometimes, they just linger, and that's enough to wear you down if you're not careful."

"You need to be alert," Mom added. "Tell your friends where you are at all times. Let someone walk you to your car at night, especially after your shifts."

"Start carrying your keys between your fingers," Dad advised. "And get that little safety alarm you clipped to your purse back in college. You still got that thing?"

"I think so," I muttered.

"Find it. And keep it on you."

"And walk with something in your hand," Mom continued. "A bat. Pepper spray. A knife—whatever you've got."

"Vivian," Dad groaned.

"I'm serious, Henry. I didn't say use it, but it's better to be ready than regretful."

"She's not wrong," he muttered. "Just don't go chasing him down with a steak knife, alright?"

"I'm not chasing anyone," I said, almost laughing. "I just want him gone."

"Then until he is," Mom said firmly, "you stay vigilant. Keep your world small and safe. Don't go anywhere unfamiliar alone. And if you even sense that something's off, you call us."

Dad hummed his agreement. "We're still on standby with the bat, by the way."

"Of course you are," I replied with a small smile tugging at my lips.

"I am proud of you, baby. For not folding. For calling. And for not letting a man with a weak backbone interrupt the woman you were becoming."

My chest swelled.

"I love you," I whispered.

"We love you more," Dad said.

The wind clawed at my coat as I turned onto my street, my breath fogging the windshield and my fingers tight on the wheel. My bag slumped in the passenger seat like it had given up hours ago. Honestly? The same.

The snow finally let up; the sky bled into dusky violet above the rooftops—soft and cold and too quiet. I pulled into my driveway slower than I needed to, the engine humming like it knew I wasn't in a rush to step back into reality.

It was a long day.

Not hard, exactly. Just long.

A lot of fake smiles. Too many awkward questions.

"You are still here?"

"Don't you have a life?"

"Girl, go home. It is Friday."

But hiding in linen-scented break rooms and reorganizing the supply closet was easier than pretending I wasn't waiting for a text that never came.

Noah didn't reach out.

And I didn't blame him. Not really.

My life had turned into a daytime soap in just a week. Surprise ex. Shaky nerves. Parental threats involving baseball bats and righteous fury. Honestly, I would have ghosted me, too.

I cut the engine off and sat in silence for a moment. Just breathing and being.

Then I glanced up.

My headlights cut across the front porch, and my heart lurched.

There was someone there.

A shadow. A figure. Standing still just left of the door.

Every muscle in my body went stiff.

No.

No.

Not again.

I gripped the steering wheel hard enough to make my knuckles ache. My breath caught. My brain raced through every possibility, already planning how fast I could reverse, whether the neighbors were home, whether I—

Then, the figure stepped forward into the glow of the porch light.

My breath released all at once.

Noah.

He was sitting on my porch steps like he was there for a while, elbows on his knees, a frown tugging at his mouth. He'd zipped up his coat, his beanie low, and his breath fogged in the cold air—but he didn't move until I was halfway up the walk.

For a second, I just stopped, and the sight of him unclenched something in me that I hadn't even realized I was holding all day. His shoulders tensed like maybe he wasn't sure if I'd be happy to see him.

I didn't move.

I just stared through the windshield, my heart still thudding in my chest, panic still draining out of my limbs.

He raised a hand in a small wave.

I forced myself to move.

Not too fast. It was not like I was hoping or praying that he would show up. Just... normal. Chill, like stepping out of my car wasn't the most significant thing I had done all day.

I tugged my coat tighter and closed the door gently, letting the sound ground me, letting my boots crunch softly against the salt and slush as I walked toward the porch and him.

For some reason, my throat went tight. Like I was holding back more than just tears, like that week—this whole chaotic, spiraling week—had finally found a crack.

His eyes were soft and a little tired. And something else I couldn't name.

I swallowed hard, blinking up at him.

"Hey," he said softly.

I breathed out. "Hey," I whispered back.

Noah watched me for a second longer. His jaw worked like he was deciding something, fighting something. Then he let out a quiet sigh, the kind that sounded like surrender or something stubborn had just given up inside him.

"I missed you," he said, his voice low and unguarded.

My breath caught. And in my head, I said what I hadn't let out loud.

You don't even know how badly I missed you.

I let out a slow and shaky breath before I closed the distance. And when I reached him, he didn't wait. He pulled me in without a word, one arm around my waist, the other curling around my shoulders, and I buried my face in his chest like it was the only place I wanted to be all day.

His lips brushed my forehead. And I sighed—finally.

Like I could exhale for the first time in hours.

"You okay?" he murmured against my hair.

"No," I said honestly. "But I will be."

His grip tightened just a little.

"You don't have to talk about it," he said. "But I am here."

"I know," I whispered. "That's why I can breathe again."

Noah exhaled through his nose, his chin resting gently on top of my head for a beat longer before he pulled back just enough to look at me. His eyes searched mine, serious then.

"Come on," he said softly. "Let's get inside. It is cold."

I nodded, and we moved together, quiet and still tangled in whatever had just passed between us. He opened the door, gently took my bag off my shoulder like it was something delicate, and helped me out of my coat like we had done it a hundred times before.

Inside, the air was warmer and softer. I tucked my gloves away while he set the cups down on the counter, already scanning the room like he was deciding what would come next.

"We can order something," he said. "Whatever you want. I don't want to assume you are up for cooking tonight."

I glanced over at him, a small smile tugging at the corner of my mouth.

"You assuming I'd cook is actually more offensive than Derek showing up."

That earned a huff of laughter from him. He shook his head and headed toward the couch.

But when we settled—me curled into the corner of the couch, him sitting close but not touching—there was a shift again, the kind we didn't have to name to feel.

"I was angry," he said quietly. "Not just because he showed up... but because I didn't know what to do with it. Seeing you talk to him. Watching him show up again and again like he still had a place there." He paused, jaw tightening. "I won't lie to you. I was jealous."

I blinked, stunned for a moment.

He lifted a hand, dragging his thumb slowly over the corner of my mouth like he was wiping away the day I had had.

"I like you, Imara," he said. No hesitation. No softening. "I like you, and I'm done pretending I don't. I won't push. But I won't let go that easily either."

He leaned in just slightly, his forehead brushing mine, his voice rough but calm.

"So if there was still something there with him—if some part of you wants to go back—tell me then. Because I can take it, I need to hear it before I fall all the way in."

My chest pulled tight. Everything in me wanted to run from its weight. But I stayed. Because Noah deserved the truth. And I had never had anyone look at me that way. Not with fear, or want, or ownership—just clarity.

"There is nothing left between Derek and me," I said, steady as I could. "Not love, hope, or even hate anymore. All that's left is a reminder of who I used to be."

His jaw twitched, but he said nothing. He was listening. He was always listening.

I stepped closer until the space between us was nothing but breath.

"You asked me to tell you before you fell," I whispered. "Noah... I already jumped."

His breath caught.

"I am all in," I added, softer now. "Whatever this is—whatever we are building—I am not scared of it. Not with you."

He blinked once like he was trying to lock the words in before they slipped away. His hand came to the side of my face, and that time, it wasn't cautious—it was confident. Certain.

He kissed me.

Not rushed. Not desperate. Just full.

Full of everything we hadn't said. Everything we had tried to hold back.

And that time?

I kissed him right back.

There was no question anymore.

Only us.

Right there.

Right then.

And everything else could wait.

CHAPTER 23: WHIPLASH

The doors slid open behind me with a familiar whoosh, spilling out a wave of fluorescent light and the low murmur of nurses changing shifts. I stepped into the crisp morning air, stretching my arms above my head until my spine cracked in five different places.

"Freedom," I muttered, letting them fall back to my sides.

Caroline followed me out, yawning so wide I could practically count her fillings. "Look at you," she teased, bumping my shoulder. "Smiling after a night shift? You're not fooling anyone."

"I'm just tired," I lied.

Caroline gave me a look. "Tired makes you cranky, not smiley. You're smiley."

I shrugged, adjusting my bag. "Maybe I'm delirious. Maybe I'm spiritually ascending. You'll never know."

Linda snorted behind us. "She's glowing."

"I'm ashy."

"Okay, but glowing under the ash."

"Goodnight," I said over my shoulder, shaking my head with a tired laugh as I waved them off. "Hope your beds are cold and your Wi-Fi's slow."

Their laughter trailed off as I made my way toward the lot. My feet dragged just a little, the weight of the last twelve hours finally settling in now that the adrenaline had worn off. But even with my back aching and my scrubs clinging in all the wrong places, I felt soft and light, like I'd been carrying a full backpack all day and had finally set it down.

I pulled my phone out of my pocket and saw the message.

Noah:

"Running a little late. Five mins max. Don't freeze."

I smiled before realizing it, tucked the phone back into my pocket, and leaned against the hospital wall, folding my arms and letting the early morning wind nip at my cheeks.

The parking lot was mostly empty then—just a few stragglers with coffee cups and slouched shoulders, the last remnants of the night shift trickling out like tired ghosts. And me—standing there in the quiet, waiting for the man who made it feel like waiting wasn't so bad.

I looked down at the slight scuff on my shoe and then toward the road.

He'd be here.

I told myself not to smile again.

I smiled anyway.

I was halfway through humming whatever melody was stuck in my head when I heard the footsteps. My smile widened. I glanced up, hopeful—thinking maybe Noah's car was just out of view, maybe he had decided to walk over instead of drive, maybe he brought one of those ridiculous muffins with the sugar crust he pretends not to like.

But it wasn't Noah.

Derek was walking toward me like he had all the time in the world and no shame in his body. His hands were in his pockets, with his hood pulled halfway up like it was some disguise.

My whole body tensed.

I pushed off the hospital wall and took one step back, then another.

I turned toward the sliding doors, ready to march right back into the safety of sterile halls, but his hand caught my arm.

My breath lodged in my throat, a short, sharp panic shooting through my chest.

"Derek," I said. "let me go."

"You were just smiling," he said softly, eyes scanning my face like he was trying to read a language he lost fluency in. "What happened?"

I stared at him. "You happened."

He frowned, confused—offended, maybe. "I'm not here to hurt you, Imara. I'm not trying to—God, why are you making it sound like I'm dangerous?"

"Because I don't want this," I snapped. "I don't want you showing up. I don't want conversations in parking lots. I don't want memories sneaking up behind me wearing your face. I'm tired, Derek."

His thumb grazed my sleeve slowly, deliberately, like we were sharing something intimate instead of me silently calculating how loud I'd have to scream to bring security running.

"I just..." His voice lowered. "I miss this."

"The way you look at me when you're mad. That little crease right here—" his hand twitched as if he was about to touch the space between my brows, "—you always got so worked up when you cared."

I flinched away, fast and sharp, as if his touch might burn through my skin. I yanked my hand back with more force this time, stepping away until there was real space between us.

His mouth curved into something between a grin and a memory as if he thought this was still charming—like we were play-acting a scene from the past.

"We used to argue like this all the time. Remember? You'd storm off, I'd chase you, and somehow, it always ended with you back in my arms. You were so fiery, so stubborn. Still are. God, I missed that."

"I know you think I'm the bad guy," he said, his voice lowering as if we were suddenly conspiring. "But you don't get to rewrite everything we had. You loved me, Imara. Deep. The kind of love people spend their whole lives looking for. And I messed up, yeah. I'll carry that. But you? You never stopped wanting me."

He leaned in, just a fraction.

"You're just scared."

Before I could even react or dig up the right words, the right shove, or the right hell no, he leaned in and kissed me.

His hand caught the side of my face as if he were in a movie and I were just supposed to melt—just supposed to fall back into something I barely survived the first time.

But I didn't melt.

I froze.

The cold and paralyzing shock hit first, but fury quickly followed, crashing in behind it like a tidal wave roaring straight through my chest.

I shoved him.

Hard.

So hard he stumbled back a step, his arms falling away as if they had never belonged there in the first place.

"What the hell is wrong with you?" I snapped, dragging the back of my hand across my mouth. "You don't get to touch me. Not now. Not ever."

He stumbled a step, looking stunned.

"You threw me away, Derek. Like I was disposable. You humiliated me, used me, lied to me—and now you show up here like you're some rewritten version of yourself, expecting what? A second chance? A damn parade?"

His face drained of color.

I laughed bitterly.

"You remember now, don't you?" My laugh was bitter. Ugly. "You blamed me for the miscarriage. Told me maybe if I hadn't been so 'emotional,' maybe if I hadn't stressed so much—"

"Imara—" he tried.

"No." My voice cut like glass. "You don't get to speak. You don't get to rewrite this into some tragic love story where we were both broken and passionate and couldn't make it work."

I stepped forward, fury building like fire under my skin. "You stormed out every time and left me. You walked away and left me to glue together every cracked piece of us alone. And now you show up here like you're some enlightened version of yourself with a new hoodie and a couple of therapy buzzwords?"

He opened his mouth again, but I was shaking now—past fury, past exhaustion.

"You're not sorry," I said, my voice trembling. "You're lonely. And I'm not your comfort object. I'm not your closure. I survived you, Derek. That doesn't mean I owe you anything."

I didn't even realize I'd balled my hands into fists until I spotted movement over his shoulder. My breath caught.

Just beyond him, across the lot—still and silent, framed in the dull orange wash of the streetlight— Noah.

He was standing at the curb, hands in his coat pockets, shoulders squared, eyes locked on me.

My stomach plummeted.

"Noah..." I whispered, my breath catching in my throat as if it were trying to choke the word back down.

He was still just standing there—still as stone, watching. And something inside me snapped into a panic.

I stepped forward fast. "Noah, wait—please—"

But he didn't wait. He turned, climbed into his truck, and slammed the door. The engine growled to life, and then he was gone, pulling out with sharp tires and brake lights that burned red through the haze of snow dust.

"Noah!" I screamed, my voice cracking into the freezing air. "Wait!"

But he was already speeding off. And the silence he left behind was louder than the truck. Something raw and ugly broke loose in my chest and spiraled too fast to catch.

"No, no, no—damn it!" I cried as I dug my phone out of my coat pocket with shaking hands, barely managing to unlock it through the blur of tears. I stabbed Charlotte's name and lifted it to my ear, my breathing ragged.

"Come get me," I croaked when she picked up. "Please. Just—come now."

I hung up before she could ask questions and used the back of my hand to wipe my face. It did nothing.

Behind me, Derek shifted, his voice low and smug. "Wow. That was dramatic."

I spun around.

"Get away from me." My voice was hoarse, cracked from the scream and the emotion strangling the rest of it.

"Come on," he said, spreading his hands like he was the victim. "You really think he would've stayed? A guy like that? All it took was one little moment, and he bolted. You sure you even knew him?"

"Shut up," I snapped, my chest heaving. "Shut up and go crawl back under whatever miserable rock you came from."

He smirked. "I mean, good riddance, right?"

I didn't answer. I couldn't. I was too busy trembling with rage and the echo of abandonment and the sting of being seen—really seen—and walked away from.

Security rounded the corner, their radios crackling as they approached.

"Is everything okay here?" one of them asked, eyes narrowing at the sight of me crying and Derek standing too close.

"She told you to leave," the second one said as he stepped in.

Derek threw up his hands, annoyed. "Alright, alright. I'm going."

He muttered something I didn't catch—didn't want to catch—and finally disappeared into the night.

I stood there alone, breath fogging in front of me, tears freezing against my skin. And even though Derek was gone, the ache in my chest felt impossibly wide.

CHAPTER 24: OF THRESHOLDS

Noah disappeared. Not in a storming-out, slamming-the-door, block-me-on-every-platform way, worse: he just stopped showing up. No more coffee waiting for me after long shifts. No more one-liner texts about the grumpy regular who tried to fight him over almond milk or quiet rides home with music low and the world feeling softer for a little while. He was gone without technically being gone. And the thing was—when someone like Noah went silent, it wasn't loud. It wasn't dramatic; it was just empty.

I found out the hard way. The humiliating way.

On day four of pretending I wasn't unraveling, I walked into the café as usual, my heart doing that hopeful-flip-stomach-drop thing I swore I was done with. But it wasn't his voice that greeted me. It was someone else's.

"Hey, Imara," one of the girls said—Jess, I think. She was wiping her hands on her apron, not meeting my eyes. Her smile stretched a little too tight. "He's in the back today."

"Oh."

That was it. Just oh. But it landed like a punch to the gut because I had heard that exact line every day that week, word for word, with the same tone and same half-apologetic glance. Which meant Noah had told them.

I nodded once, pretending like it was nothing. Like I hadn't called and texted him or stared at my phone at 3 a.m. as if it might suddenly light up and explain everything. I ordered a tea I didn't even want and sat in the corner like a ghost in my own life. And still—he never came out.

I told myself it was fine. I would have thought the worst; hell, I did. But that didn't stop it from hurting. It didn't stop the ache in my chest or the sting behind my eyes every time I reached for my phone and remembered, again, that he hadn't reached back. I was angry. Because he didn't even give me the benefit of the doubt or text me to say, "Was that what it looks like?" or "Do you want to explain?" He just disappeared, folded in on himself, and left me standing in the fallout as if I had somehow lit the match.

I sat on my couch in pajama pants and a sweatshirt that didn't even belong to me anymore—it was passed around the friend group too many times to claim ownership—and I watched the wind press against the windows like it was trying to come in. My scarf was still by the door; wrapping it around my face wouldn't protect me from this heartbreak anyway.

The girls were all there. Like they always were. Caroline clutched a pint of rocky road as if it held answers. Linda had tissues in one hand, a nail polish brush in the other, and a smutty romance novel balanced precariously on her thigh. Charlotte twisted her curls into the messiest braid I had ever seen while narrating a soap opera version of my life with full conviction and zero accuracy. And somehow, it helped.

I looked at those ridiculous, loyal, chaos-ridden women, and I imagined staying—really staying here in Vermont. Not just visiting or passing through on the way to whatever was next but building something that lasted—putting down roots.

But then that voice crept in. Or maybe I just went home, back to the place where everything made sense before it all fell apart. Back to my parent's house and my old room, where the wallpaper still peeled in the corner, and my mom insisted on folding my laundry as if I were still sixteen. Where my mom made dinner before I asked, and my dad wouldn't let me leave the driveway without checking my tires; back to being the daughter, the recovering, the starting over—again.

Back to that hospital where every corner held a memory I didn't want to revisit. Where my traitorous best friend still walked the halls as if nothing had happened and where my name was whispered more than spoken because people gossiped about drama more than they loved truth.

Or maybe I left again, kept moving, and chasing another temporary contract and a clean slate. Uprooted myself every time the soil started to settle, just to prove I could. Just to outrun the part of me that still didn't trust good things to stay.

Because look how fast it unraveled here. A man I hadn't asked for. A kiss I hadn't wanted. A goodbye that didn't even get said out loud. Now I was crying into my couch pillow like I hadn't evolved one inch since twenty-one-year-old Imara got her heart dragged through the dirt.

I knew better. But it still hurt like hell.

Charlotte threw a kernel of popcorn at me. "Are you crying or just dehydrated?"

I sniffed. "Both."

"You need electrolytes and closure," she said, completely serious. "And maybe a new man."

Caroline groaned from under her blanket. "No more men. Let's get her a cat. Or a sword."

"Or a cat with a sword," Linda added, deadpan, flipping a page in her book.

I was sniffling into a paper towel and eating dry cereal straight from the box as if it were a form of therapy. It crunched loudly in my mouth, competing with the sound of Caroline digging around in a bag of gummy worms like she was mining for treasure.

No one spoke for a minute. Not really. We were all just... there. Existing in the aftermath.

"So," Linda finally said, her voice gentle, "are we gonna talk about it? The fact that Derek kissed you without permission? That's not a misunderstanding, Imara. That's borderline assault."

I pressed the paper towel tighter to my face, nodding slowly. "I know. I—I've been thinking about it."

Charlotte frowned. "Are you gonna press charges?"

"I don't know," I whispered. "Part of me wants to, and parts of me wants him gone for good."

"He shouldn't get to make you feel unsafe and then walk away like it was nothing," Caroline muttered, popping a gummy worm into her mouth and chewing as if it were personal. "People like that depend on you brushing it off. Don't."

I nodded again, my throat tight. Then I took a breath I didn't really want to take and said the thing that was crawling around my chest for days.

"My mom wants me to come home."

All three heads snapped toward me as if I had just threatened to set the couch on fire.

"I'm not saying I will," I added quickly. "I'm just—wondering. If I should. Things are a mess. Maybe I'm just dragging it out here."

Caroline's hand shot up. "Okay, no. Absolutely not."

Linda nodded, dead serious. "No more sarcastic night shifts. No more spontaneous dance breaks in the meds closet. No more dragging me out of patient flirting disasters."

Charlotte sighed dramatically and patted my foot. "You can't leave. We've already decided. You live here now."

I barely laughed, but it cracked through the ache. "I didn't know I meant that much to y'all."

"You do," Charlotte said, real quiet now. "You changed this place, Imara. We're happier."

I blinked. But she wasn't done.

"You came in like this hurricane in scrubs," she said, eyes locked on mine, "and somehow you made everything lighter. Even the heavy stuff. You made this town feel alive again. You made us feel like we had someone in our corner who actually sees people. Who actually stays."

I pressed my lips together, but it was already happening—the sting behind my eyes, the wobble in my chin.

"And I don't say this kind of stuff often," she went on, her voice softer now, "but we've got you. All of us. You're not just some friend who floated in and disappeared when things got too hard. You're ours, Imara. And we're yours."

She reached out, wrapping her fingers around my hand like they were anchors.

"You don't have to fight alone anymore. Not here. Not ever again."

Linda nodded, her mascara already smudging a little as she wiped her eyes with a tissue.

"We've got your back. Always."

Caroline sat up straighter under the blanket as if she were about to declare war.

"Ride-or-die, bury-the-body type loyalty. I mean it. You say the word, and Derek's social security number is mine."

That made me laugh—a real laugh this time.

But Charlotte just squeezed my hand tighter.

"You don't have to earn our love. You don't have to fix everything to deserve to stay. We want you here because we love you. Because you're enough. Even when you're a mess. Especially then."

A single tear slid down my cheek before I could stop it, and I didn't wipe it away.

"I've never had that," I whispered. "Not like this."

"Well," Charlotte said, letting her forehead rest gently against mine, "get used to it. You're stuck with us now."

I blinked fast and nodded as if that would stop the sting behind my eyes.

We ended up huddled together, three blankets deep, a tangle of limbs while old episodes played low on the TV.

A knock startled me, and my heart launched itself to my throat.

I sat up fast—too fast—instead, nearly launching Caroline off the couch in the process.

She squawked, limbs flailing under the blanket. "Ma'am—?"

I didn't answer. I was already halfway across the room, praying it would be Noah—praying it would be him.

I rushed to the door, adrenaline pumping, my stomach a tight, painful knot of nerves and hope. My fingers fumbled with the lock, and I yanked the door open.

"I just need a minute."

Linda shot up off the couch, grabbing the closest thing within reach—which happened to be a throw pillow—and raised it as if it were a weapon.

Caroline kicked off the blanket, her eyes wild, halfway into fight mode with a spoon still clutched in her fist. Charlotte was already halfway to the door, her expression dark.

"You've got three seconds to back off before we call your mother and the local priest," she declared.

"Guys," I said sharply, holding up my hand, "I've got this."

Charlotte glared at me as if she wanted to disagree but trusted me enough to step back.

I looked at Derek, meeting his eyes dead on.

"You have ten seconds before I call the police," I warned.

"I just need a minute," he replied quickly, his hands raised in faux surrender.

"No," I said, my voice clipped and exhausted. "You've had minutes. You've had hours. You've had years."

But he stepped forward just enough to cross the line of space I had drawn in my head, just enough that I had to listen.

"Be with me," he said, quiet, measured, desperate. "Let me fix this. I know I can. Just… come back with me."

I didn't even flinch. I turned around.

"I'm calling the cops."

That made him panic.

"Wait—wait," he pleaded.

I paused—not for him, but because I needed to catch my breath before I lost it.

"I can't go back to Virginia," he blurted.

"Not yet. Maybe not ever," I replied, and something in my chest went cold.

"What?" I asked.

"I got into some stuff," Derek said, his voice low, "after Tania. After everything. Nothing huge at first—just bad decisions. I burned some bridges and borrowed money I couldn't pay back. But then one thing led to another. I got hurt. I owed the wrong people. I... stopped showing up to work. They let me go. I messed up some contracts—I burned bridges. I'm being sued, Imara."

He swallowed hard, his eyes flicking up to meet mine.

"I lost the apartment last month. I've been sleeping in my car."

"Derek—" I began, but he interrupted.

"I'm not asking you to take me back," he said quickly, holding up his hands. "I know you've moved on. I saw it, okay? That guy—the way he looks at you. It's done. I get it."

"Then why are you here?" I whispered, my throat tight, my fingers trembling on the edge of the door.

He hesitated, and the air between us grew sharp.

"Because I didn't know where else to go," he admitted, his voice breaking just a little this time. "I tried to fix it. I swear. I went back to my parents for a while, but they kicked me out. My brother won't answer my calls."

He pressed his knuckles to his forehead. "It's bad. I had two clients threaten legal action, and another one already filed. One of them is talking about damages. There's a lien on my accounts. I might lose everything."

I froze because even after everything, I still recognized that tone in his voice—desperation, real, and raw.

I went still.

He looked up, his eyes rimmed with exhaustion.

"I wasn't thinking clearly. I was trying to rebuild my portfolio, and I overpromised. I took on more than I could handle. I panicked. And I—I signed a lease on a studio space I couldn't afford, thinking I'd get a loan to float me through. The loan didn't come through."

He exhaled shakily. "Everything I had is gone. My car, my apartment, my clients. I'm living in a friend's guest room, and they want me to be out next week. I've been trying to get to Vermont for days, but I kept sleeping in rest stops because I couldn't afford gas in one go."

He wasn't lying.

But I wasn't the same woman who had dropped everything to fix a man who broke me.

And I was sure as hell not about to put the life I was rebuilding on pause to save someone who had watched me drown and handed me an anchor.

"I'm sorry," I said because I meant it. "But I'm not your lifeboat anymore."

"I'm not asking you to fix it," he murmured. "Just... don't shut the door all the way. Please, Imara."

"Please, Imara."

I closed my eyes, and for a second, I was back in Virginia.

Back in that expensive apartment, back when I thought love meant sacrificing everything—even myself. Back when I thought the right and hard things were always the same.

But that wasn't then. And I wasn't her.

I was a woman standing at a door she had finally built for herself. I was a woman who knew what it meant to lose everything and still choose herself repeatedly.

And yet, Derek might have been telling the truth.

Noah might have walked away.

And there was no version of this where I got to keep them both.

So I didn't answer.

Not with a yes. Not with a no. I just stood there, holding the weight of it all in my chest because I didn't know the right choice.

I just knew it was going to cost me something.

And that was where it ended.

Not with a kiss.

Not with a reunion.

Not with a happy ending tied in a bow.

Just me.

A woman in a doorway, deciding if kindness meant losing herself again—or standing firm in the life she had finally claimed.

📖 Loved the Story? There's More Waiting for You...

If Imara's journey touched something deep in you—
If you found yourself holding your breath during the quiet
moments,
Or whispering *"same"* after a line that hit a little too close—

Then you belong with us.

👉 **Visit** https://wrongblacklove.com/join-the-journey/ to:

– Get exclusive story extras not in the book

– Be the first to know when the next chapter drops

– Read behind-the-scenes notes and bonus scenes

– Join a community of readers who feel the same things you do

Your next favorite moment is waiting.

Don't miss it.

Visit Now → https://wrongblacklove.com/join-the-journey/

 Or scan the QR code below:

www.ingramcontent.com/pod-product-compliance
Lightning Source LLC
Chambersburg PA
CBHW071248250626

47163CB00002B/375